THE MAGICAL

GW01185304

Double
BOOKED

LIZ HEDGECOCK

WHITE
RHINO
BOOKS

For John,
who keeps me on the right lines

Chapter 1

Jemma watched the pendulum of the grandfather clock swing backwards and forwards, backwards and forwards. *If I'm not careful*, she thought, *I'll fall asleep right here, at the counter.*

It was almost twelve o'clock, and so far they had had one proper customer. A smart man with a brass-buttoned blazer and a rolled umbrella had strolled in, tipped his hat, and stated precisely what he wanted, down to which edition and bindings he was prepared to accept. Maddy had known exactly what he meant, located the book in the designated area of the stockroom, and brought it out in its protective box for inspection. The customer had pronounced himself satisfied, paid the price asked, and left with the box under his arm. He had not browsed, he had not asked about any other books, and Maddy had not attempted to sell him any.

Apart from that customer, perhaps five people had walked in, gazed blankly at the rows of books behind glass, and left. One couple had whispered, 'It looks expensive, doesn't it?' and scurried out with a fearful glance at the counter, as if Jemma might coerce them into buying something.

'Is it usually this quiet on a Monday?' she asked Maddy.

Maddy tore her gaze from the copy of the *Bookseller's Companion* which she was perusing, and considered. 'This is normal,' she said, eventually. 'This isn't the sort of bookshop where we have lots of casual browsers. People who come to BJF Antiquarian Books tend to know exactly what they want.'

'I can see that,' said Jemma, remembering the man with the umbrella. 'I'm just used to things being busier.'

'You worked in a general bookshop, didn't you?' Maddy asked, with a slightly pitying note in her voice.

'Yes, I managed a general bookshop,' Jemma replied. 'We had people coming in all the time.'

Maddy shuddered visibly. 'Churn,' she said, almost to herself. 'People picking up the books, and putting down the books, and – and *touching* the books.' She rubbed her thumb and forefinger together, then returned to her magazine.

The clock struck twelve like a death knell.

'I think I'll take my lunch,' said Jemma, 'if that's OK.'

'Yes, of course,' said Maddy, without looking up. 'You're the boss.'

Yes, I am, thought Jemma, in an attempt to convince

herself. She got her bag, put on her jacket, and set off along the road. She walked quickly, partly because it was chilly out, but also because she didn't want to waste more of her hour away from the shop than she had to. A couple of minutes later she pushed open the familiar door, and walked into Burns Books.

Raphael was reclining in the armchair, his fingertips on his temples, and Luke stood nearby. Folio sat on the counter between two boxes of books, watching them both. 'Let's try again,' said Raphael. 'Visualise horror books. Tell yourself that the shop needs horror books.'

Luke screwed his face up. If anything, he looked constipated. 'All right,' he said, after a minute or so, 'I've got it.' He strode towards the stockroom with purpose and returned with another box of books. But when he opened it, it was full of Harlequin romances. 'I don't believe it!' he cried. 'What am I doing wrong?'

Raphael laughed. 'Jemma, why don't you try.'

'Horror books,' said Jemma. 'We need horror stories.' She walked to the stockroom, selected a random box, and brought it back. But when she opened it, the box was full of books about business management.

'While I regard that as a horror story,' said Raphael, 'I doubt most of our customers would agree.' He looked from Jemma to Luke. 'I suspect you both have something on your mind.' He eyed the box of romance novels, then Luke, who appeared, for him, decidedly pink.

'I'm thinking about – putting myself out there,' he said. 'It's been a long time since I felt – well, in that frame of mind. But now I've got a stable job...'

'You mean dating?' asked Jemma.

Luke fidgeted with a black shirt button. 'I suppose I do,' he said. 'Obviously it's a bit different when you're undead.'

'I imagine it would be,' said Jemma. 'Do you only date other vampires?'

'It would make things easier,' said Luke. 'But I'm open to new experiences.' He fidgeted some more. 'I've downloaded an app.'

Raphael rolled his eyes.

'Don't be like that,' said Luke. 'I haven't opened it yet. I'm waiting for when things . . . you know, feel right.'

'Checking it out can't hurt,' said Jemma. 'I mean, romance is clearly on your mind.' She nodded towards the boxes, and Luke looked rather resentful.

'And what about you?' he asked, indicating the box of business books. 'Trouble in paradise?'

'No,' said Jemma, drawing herself up to her full height, which was still not enough to be remotely on a level with Luke. Then she sighed, and slumped. 'It's just so boring. Hardly anyone comes in, the people who do normally run straight out again because the shop scares them, and Maddy is perfectly capable of dealing with any actual customers. It's barely worth me being there.'

'I did say,' Raphael remarked, mildly, 'that it doesn't have to stay an antiquarian bookshop.'

'I know,' said Jemma. *But I'm worried*, she added to herself. *I'm worried that if I change things it won't work, and I'll have messed up a perfectly good bookshop because I didn't understand it.* 'I guess it's early days,' she said. 'I'm still wondering what to do for the best.'

'That's very cautious of you,' said Raphael. 'Anyway, I'm pleased that your bookshop is quiet at the moment. It means we have more time to think about the Assistant Keeper problem.'

Jemma blinked. 'I actually came over to get lunch,' she said.

'And Carl being downstairs is incidental,' said Raphael, with a twinkle.

Jemma smiled. 'Don't tell him that his cappuccino's the main attraction, will you?' And with that she escaped before any more awkward questions could be asked.

As usual at this time, the large lower bookshop was busy. Customers roamed around the shelves, not quite small enough to be ants in the lofty vaulted space of the shop, but with similar levels of scurrying and industry. Carl himself was dealing with a sizeable queue, making coffees, warming paninis, and exchanging friendly banter with their regulars. It was odd but nice to see him absorbed, not conscious of her. His twists had grown; they stuck straight up from his scalp, maybe an inch and a half now. *Has he redone them? I see him almost every day. Why haven't I noticed?* Then Carl caught sight of her and waved.

Jemma waved back, then walked over to General Fiction and picked up a Wodehouse she hadn't read, *Pigs Have Wings*, to keep her company in the queue. *Not that I'm trying to avoid thinking about the other shop*, she told herself. *I'm being productive and making the best use of my lunch hour.*

When she reached the front of the queue, Carl grinned at her. 'Cappuccino, I presume?'

'Yes please, and a tomato and mozzarella panini.'

'Eat in or take out?' Then his grin narrowed a little. 'You OK?'

She frowned. 'Yes, of course I am. Why wouldn't I be?'

He turned away to put the panini in the warmer, and began making her cappuccino. When he finally put her cup on the counter, he wore the expression of someone walking across ice. 'You just looked a little too pleased to see me.' His gaze moved to the book in her hand. 'And you've got a PG Wodehouse book. You told me once that you read those for escapism.'

Jemma sighed. 'Well done, Sherlock Holmes,' she said. 'It's probably nothing.'

'Doesn't look like nothing,' said Carl. 'I've got rehearsals with Rumpus tonight, but we could go out later, maybe nine? Or I could come round?'

Jemma heard a voice behind her mutter, 'Oh *do* get a move on.'

'No, it's fine,' she said quickly. 'Like I said, it's probably nothing.'

Jemma paid, took her cappuccino and found a small table at the edge of the café area. She opened her book and attempted to lose herself in it, but she had only read two pages when the cry of 'Tomato and mozzarella panini!' brought her back into the café.

The panini was nice, and so was the cappuccino, and the bookshop had just the right soothing background hum; but somehow the image of a bookshop, empty apart from herself and Maddy, and silent apart from the ticking of the grandfather clock, kept getting between her and the Empress of Blandings. Once she had finished her lunch Jemma sighed again, though she wasn't sure exactly why, and took her book upstairs.

'Luke's on his lunch,' said Raphael. He hadn't moved from the armchair, but Folio was sitting on his lap. 'You can serve yourself, can't you?'

Jemma laughed. 'Yeah.' She popped behind the counter, scanned her book with the little scan gun they now had at each till, and held her phone to the card reader. 'All done.'

'Oh yes,' said Raphael. 'I put a book aside for you. I was shelving your boxes and I thought it might be useful.'

Jemma saw a Burns Books paper bag on the counter, with a book inside. She drew it out. *Your Business, Your Way*. 'Oh, um, thanks,' she said. 'Do you think it'll help?'

'Well, you don't seem happy with things as they are,' said Raphael. 'You can always bring it back.'

'I suppose I can,' said Jemma, still gazing at the cover of the book. 'I'll start it tonight. Thanks, Raphael.' She replaced the book in the bag, added the Wodehouse to it, and left the shop.

She still had ten minutes of her lunch hour left, so she stopped in at Nafisa's mini-market and bought a packet of sausages and enough potatoes to make a generous portion of mash for one. *I don't have to impress anyone tonight,* she thought. *And if I'm seriously taking on Brian's bookshop – no, not Brian's bookshop, my bookshop – I need proper food.*

Nafisa frowned at the packet of sausages. 'Are you sure?' she said.

'You're selling them,' said Jemma. 'I assume they're fit for human consumption.'

Nafisa considered her. 'Sausages don't seem very you,' she said. 'You're more chickpeas and lentils these days.'

'Don't forget the quinoa,' said Jemma. 'Yes, I suppose I am. But sometimes you need comfort food.'

Nafisa let out an ominous 'Mmm,' and scanned the sausages. 'May you find comfort in them,' she said, almost as if she were blessing them, and handed them to Jemma. And as Jemma strolled back to BJF Antiquarian Books, opened the door, and saw Maddy sitting just as she had left her an hour before, she really hoped that she would.

Chapter 2

Jemma leaned against the worktop in Brian's – no, *her* – compact but well-appointed kitchen, reading *Your Business, Your Way*. In the background, sausages sizzled. Every so often she would reach across and poke them with a spatula to ensure they cooked evenly. But really, her attention was on the book.

They had closed on the stroke of five, and the afternoon had been as quiet as the morning. They had cashed up at a quarter to five, since Maddy had said with authority that none of their regulars were likely to visit after four thirty anyway, and locked the takings in the safe, ready to go to the bank tomorrow. The takings were fairly respectable, considering the low number of books they had sold. 'Low volume, high profit,' Maddy had said, with a smug air. There was no tidying to do, no books to replace on shelves, and nothing to be said about the day at all. 'See you tomorrow,' said Maddy, and left on the first chime of the clock.

Jemma enjoyed mashing her potatoes. She added plenty of milk and butter, and pretended that she was pummelling the bookshop into shape. *Yes*, she thought, as she mashed, *it's my bookshop, and it is up to me to make the changes.* Perhaps she had mashed the potatoes too thoroughly and added a little too much milk, since she was left with a purée instead of a mash, and when she stuck her three sausages into it at jaunty angles, they immediately sank into the puddle of potato. Jemma refused to derive an insight from this minor cookery fail, adding a dollop of tomato ketchup and telling herself that it would taste fine. Who wanted hard lumpy mash, anyway?

She continued to flick through the book as she ate. It was rather inspiring, with its talk of working out your goals and moulding your business to fit them, and ensuring that the business reflected your values. But while it was heavy on buzzwords, it was extremely light on practicalities. It didn't, for example, tell you what to do if you had taken on a bookshop which was the exact opposite of a shop you would actually want to visit, complete with an assistant who was happy with things the way they were. Jemma laid the book down, and decided to focus on her remaining sausage rather than her values.

She was just chewing the last mouthful, and wishing that Carl was there to laugh over the book with her, when her mobile rang. Jemma's heart leapt. Maybe his rehearsal had finished early and they could go out for that drink after all. But when she got her phone from her jacket pocket the display said *Mum*.

Jemma's heart sank a little, which made her feel guilty, and she pressed *Answer*. 'Hi, Mum.'

'Hello, Jemma. I didn't expect you to answer.' Her mother sounded a little aggrieved that she had. 'I thought you'd still be working. Or on your way home.'

'It's gone half past seven, Mum. Don't forget I live over the bookshop now.'

'Oh yes.' Her mother sniffed. 'I always liked that other flat. Such a nice building. And a nice road, too.'

As far as Jemma could remember, her mother had visited the flat twice, and hadn't been particularly complimentary on either occasion. 'Expensive, though,' she said. 'This one is rent-free. Perk of the job.'

'Probably because the owner can't find a tenant for it,' said her mother. 'Anyway, how are you getting on with your new job?'

Wild horses wouldn't have dragged the truth out of Jemma. 'It's great,' she said. 'The shop has so much potential, and I'm looking forward to making changes.'

'I expect the owner will have things to say about that.'

'Oh no, he supports me fully,' said Jemma.

'Well, it's his money.' Her mother sighed. 'If the bookshop was failing anyway, anything is an improvement.'

'It's only your positive attitude that keeps me going, Mum,' said Jemma.

'I'm sorry, I missed that,' said her mother. 'I wish you'd get a proper phone line. I'm sure phoning your mobile is costing me a fortune. Anyway, your boss. Is he nice?'

Jemma felt on firm ground now. 'Yes, he's very nice.'

'And how old is he, would you say?'

Jemma couldn't help grinning. 'Oh, he's much older than me.' She would have loved to see her mother's face if she had told her *how* much older Raphael was, but sadly it was not to be.

'Oh,' said her mother. 'I suppose at least if you don't have to commute you'll have time to go out and meet people. And I'm sure lots of nice people come into the bookshop.'

'Mum, I'm seeing someone,' said Jemma. 'I did tell you.' She had found more and more, since leaving home, that her mother's brain was like a temperamental sieve. It was good at retaining the things she wanted to remember, and remarkably skilled at letting everything else go.

'Did you? Are you sure? What does he do? I suppose it is a he. Or should I say they? Is that what one says now?'

'He's a he,' said Jemma. 'He works—' She hesitated. But working in the café was nothing to be ashamed of. 'He's working in the main bookshop café at the moment, because he's between jobs. He's an actor.'

'Oh,' said her mother. 'Does he have a name, this actor? Would I have seen him in anything?'

'I doubt it, Mum, he hasn't done any TV work. His name is Carl.'

Her mother sniffed in a way that suggested that if Carl hadn't been on her television, he didn't really exist. 'Amanda and Jake have bought the house they were looking at, in the next village.'

'Oh yes, she texted,' said Jemma. 'I know they really wanted it.' Amanda was two years younger than Jemma, and somehow, since Jemma had left home to go to university and Amanda had decided to live at home and become a primary school teacher, Jemma felt the balance of her mother's affection had distinctly shifted in Amanda's favour. Amanda's career was so rewarding; Amanda's boyfriend Jake had such lovely manners; Amanda came for Sunday lunch every weekend without fail. Jemma probably would have resented her sister if Amanda hadn't been so frank in private about how hard she found teaching some days, and how often their mother praised Jemma to her as an independent woman making her own way in the world.

'Yes,' said her mother. 'I'm so pleased they've been able to get a foot on the property ladder.'

'Oh, absolutely,' said Jemma. 'And with the money I'm saving on rent at the moment, hopefully I can get a deposit together for when I'm ready to buy.'

'Does this Carl have a place of his own?' asked her mother, in a voice which somehow suggested a dragon scenting an addition to her hoard.

Jemma laughed. 'He works in the shop café, Mum, what do you think?'

'I only asked,' said her mother. 'Anyway, I'd better go; *EastEnders* is on soon.' Jemma had a distinct suspicion that, though her mother must have visited London several times, she still thought *EastEnders* was an entirely accurate representation of the whole of London life. She considered asking if she had seen *Notting Hill*, then decided that would just bring a whole new range of assumptions to deal with.

'It's been nice talking to you, Mum,' she said. 'Are you all right? And how about Dad?'

'Oh yes, we're both fine,' said her mother. 'Your father is building the Millennium Falcon at the moment. It's all over the dining-room table.'

Jemma grinned. Dad had always been a Lego fanatic, building things for them when they were tiny, then with them, and when Jemma and Amanda reached their teenage years and preferred hanging around the local shopping centre, without them. 'I'm sure it won't take him long to finish it,' she said.

'You haven't seen it,' her mother said, darkly. 'Anyway, it's five to eight and I've just got time to make a cup of tea, so I must go. I'll phone you next week, Jemma.'

'OK. Bye, Mum,' said Jemma. And as always, her mother managed to put the phone down first.

Jemma looked at the phone in her hand. As usual, her mother had said nothing about her own life. Jemma occasionally wondered whether her mother could be a secret operative for MI5, or engaged in a string of glamorous affairs. She was certainly good at gathering information while managing to divulge only select snippets of her own.

Jemma sighed. *Even if she did have an amazing secret life*, she thought, *I still wouldn't want to be my mum. She's so – so determined to be disappointed. Particularly in me.* She knew full well that even if she made the bookshop into the most high-profile, successful bookshop in London –

no, the world – and earned a six-figure salary, and married Carl, who then landed a leading role in *EastEnders*, her mother would find something to be disappointed about. But she still wanted to please her.

I'll make a go of this bookshop, she thought, and her hand tightened on the phone. *I'll work out my goals, and my vision, and my values, and I'll make that shop into a place where I'm proud and happy to work. And if Maddy doesn't like it, well—* She shrugged. *She can put up, or shut up.*

Jemma nodded, to bed in her resolve more deeply, fetched her laptop, and went into the kitchen to make tea and raid the emergency biscuits. Perhaps, if she could transform the bookshop into the shop of her dreams, everything else would follow. At any rate, it was worth a try.

Chapter 3

Jemma's resolve to take the bookshop in hand was still firm when she woke in the morning. She had created a new spreadsheet the previous evening: colour-coded, with goals, milestones, and dependencies. That had made her feel much better. When Carl texted at nine o'clock, she had replied: *Yes, I'm fine, I've got a plan.* She hadn't even read herself to sleep with *Pigs Have Wings*, because she had no need to escape any more.

When getting ready, she selected comparatively businesslike attire: black trousers, a smart top, and a jacket instead of her usual cardigan. She thought of Maddy's Birkenstocks, and added a pair of shoes with a slight heel. After all, now that she spent most of her time sitting, baseball boots weren't required. Thus armoured, she made herself a strong coffee, tucked her laptop under her arm, and went downstairs.

She almost jumped out of her skin when Maddy arrived five minutes later, and only just managed to swallow her mouthful of coffee. 'You're . . . early,' she said, and felt her resolve trickling away. She put her mug down and sat up straight.

'Not really,' said Maddy, hanging up her coat and beret. Jemma eyed her feet and wondered whether the Birkenstocks would persist throughout the winter, and what Maddy would do if it snowed. 'I always come in early on the third Tuesday of the month. It's stocktake day.'

'Stocktake day?' said Jemma, feeling like an inadequate echo.

'Yes, Brian and I always went through the stock and checked that our flagship books were in good condition, and then he would review his acquisition plan,' said Maddy.

'Oh,' said Jemma. 'I see. Um . . . is there a system?'

'Oh yes,' said Maddy. 'We developed it together. It is quite complicated, but I can explain it to you if you like.' Her expression was kind.

'That would be . . . great,' said Jemma. She cast an imploring look at her laptop, begging her action plan to save her, and saw the little power light blink off. With that, the last of her resolve dribbled from the toes of her modestly heeled shoes.

'I'll make myself a drink,' said Maddy, 'then we can get started.'

At that moment Jemma's phone rang. The display said *Burns Books*. 'I have to take this,' she said. 'Hello, Jemma James speaking.'

'Oh, hello Jemma,' said Raphael, sounding surprised. 'I don't suppose you could pop round? I'm having a spot of trouble and I'd welcome your advice.'

Jemma could have kissed the phone. 'Of course, I'll come now.' She ended the call. 'I'm sorry, Maddy, but something's come up at Burns Books. I'm afraid I'll have to leave you to it.' A sudden evil impulse led her to add, 'Will you be able to manage on your own?'

Maddy's face was absolutely expressionless. 'Oh yes,' she said.

'In that case,' said Jemma, 'I'll get going.' And she shrugged into her jacket with a distinct sense of being let off the hook.

Jemma was almost at the bookshop when she began to wonder what the trouble might be. Had Folio gone on the rampage? Was the shop throwing a tantrum? At least it was too early to be customer-related. She found lights on when she arrived, and Luke sitting behind the counter, engrossed in *The Rules Of Dating*. 'Oh, hi,' he said. 'Raphael's downstairs. Everything's in hand.'

'Is it?' Jemma glanced about her for signs of trouble, but none were apparent. The only difference from usual was that Luke had had a haircut, and his normally shaggy hair was neatly combed. It made him look as if he were in his late teens. 'Doing research?'

Luke lowered the book. 'Yes, I am,' he said. 'I'm going to a – a thing tonight, and I thought it best to be prepared.'

'A thing?' said Jemma. 'What sort of thing?'

'Speed dating,' said Luke. 'Downstairs at the Rat and Compasses. It starts quite early, so I'm going straight from work.'

'Oh,' said Jemma. 'Well, good luck.' All sorts of questions were on the tip of her tongue, but she suspected she might not want to know the answers. 'I'd better go and see what Raphael wants.'

Downstairs, Raphael was sitting at one of the café tables, with a takeaway coffee cup from Rolando's and a large notepad in front of him. 'I need help,' he said. 'I'm stuck.'

Jemma sat opposite him and turned the notepad to see what he had written. At the top were the words *Assistant Keeper: Westminster* in Raphael's beautiful copperplate hand, and the rest of the page was blank.

'I see,' she said. 'Let's start at the beginning. Is the role permanent, or temporary?'

Raphael frowned. 'It's sort of both. It's permanent if you can manage to hold on to it, and temporary if you can't.'

Jemma sighed. 'Maybe put "to be confirmed". Who does the role report to?'

'Oh, that's easy,' said Raphael, looking much happier. 'The role reports to me. Keeper of England.' He passed Jemma his pen.

'OK,' said Jemma, writing it down. 'Salary?'

'Ooooh, I know this!' cried Raphael. 'One thousand guineas per annum.'

Jemma's pen froze above the paper, and she stared at him. 'A thousand guineas?'

'Yes,' said Raphael. 'It's a nice round sum, that's why I remembered it.'

'Is that all?' asked Jemma.

'There are some special allowances,' said Raphael. 'One's expenses are paid, for example.'

'What sort of expenses?'

'Well, you know.' Raphael shifted in his seat. 'Expenses incurred in the course of performing one's duty. So if one happened to be at a meeting, and one required sustenance…'

Jemma grinned. 'So all those coffees and pastries from Rolando's go on expenses?'

Raphael shrugged. 'Completely necessary,' he said. 'I've never had any trouble getting them signed off. And of course there is the book budget, which in the case of agreed acquisitions is unlimited.'

'I see.' Jemma thought for a moment. 'And Gertrude?'

'Company car,' said Raphael.

Jemma wrote: *Plus generous expenses including subsistence and company car.* 'Pension?'

'Nooooo,' said Raphael, as if the idea were ridiculous. And now that Jemma thought about it, a pension scheme for staff who were presumably immortal *was* rather unrealistic.

'OK, got that,' she said. 'What about hours?'

'Flexible,' said Raphael. 'But on call for twenty-four hours, seven days a week.'

'Really?' said Jemma.

'Oh yes,' said Raphael. 'Keepers never sleep. Well, obviously we do, but in an emergency—'

'I get it.' Jemma considered the sheet of paper. 'How would you summarise the job?'

Raphael drank some coffee, then sat back in his chair and closed his eyes. Jemma was just debating whether to poke him when he sat bolt upright. 'The Assistant Keeper of Westminster,' he declared, 'is responsible for maintaining the knowledge sources in their care in good condition, and for acquiring new assets with the agreement of their superiors. They are also responsible for preventing any knowledge-related emergencies in the borough of Westminster, and if any do occur, containing same without involving outside agencies or the media.'

'Hang on a minute,' muttered Jemma, busy scribbling. 'You're asking them to do that for a thousand pounds a year?'

'Guineas,' Raphael corrected. 'Plus allowances.'

'Good luck with that,' said Jemma. 'OK, let's go to qualifications and experience.'

'Hmm,' said Raphael, stretching his legs out beneath the table. 'The most important is that they must be able to read.'

Jemma laughed. 'I would have thought that went without saying.'

'Ah, someone got past me in 1850,' said Raphael. 'He lasted a good three months. Oh yes, and they need to be able to write, too.'

'What about actual qualifications?' said Jemma.

Raphael looked nonplussed. 'That's a bit tricky,' he said. 'You see, not all of us have had what you might call a formal education.'

Jemma decided not to ask for clarification. 'All right, what about experience?'

'We don't ask for too much at this level,' said Raphael. 'This is a relatively junior position, so we'd be looking for a minimum of ten years running a book-heavy environment with no major incidents. We'd also be prepared to consider people with twenty years experience and one successfully contained major incident.' He smiled. 'In some ways those candidates are better, because they've had firsthand experience of disaster management. Oh yes, you can put that. Non-accountable involvement in one disaster or three minor incidents, with no loss of assets. Oh, or life.'

Jemma sighed, and wrote. 'Anything else? Business experience?'

Raphael laughed. 'You've worked with me, Jemma, what do you think?'

Jemma put her pen down. 'If you can fill in the basic duties of the post, that's more or less it for the job description,' she said. 'And you can work out the experience and the qualities you want.'

'Oh yes,' said Raphael. 'Not like Brian. That's mainly why I'm doing this, so that I don't end up with another one of him.'

'So how does the recruitment process work?' said Jemma.

'Oh, we always have lots of candidates,' said Raphael. 'I normally tell them to bring three books, shove them in a room together, and see who's left at the end.'

Jemma remembered the graduate scheme recruitment processes she had gone through, and revised her opinion of them to actually quite humane. 'What about the people who don't make it?'

'Oh, they can always try again,' said Raphael. 'They generally find a home somewhere. Many of them end up working in normal bookshops. Mostly, you see, they just like books, and the rest of it is a bit of an add-on.'

'As opposed to the people who think they'll be working in a normal bookshop, then find out that isn't the case,' said Jemma. 'OK, so once you've added the duties and written the person spec, you advertise the job somewhere appropriate. I'd suggest for a role like this that you should have a closing date of three weeks to a month from the date you post the advert—'

'A month?' Raphael's eyebrows were almost in his hairline.

'Yes,' said Jemma.

'And where do I advertise?' said Raphael. 'I was planning to mention it to my staff and see who was up for it.'

'And then put them all in a room, I suppose,' said Jemma.

'Of course,' said Raphael. 'How else am I meant to pick someone?'

'You remember when I made you interview me?' said Jemma.

'But that was different,' said Raphael. 'That was for the bookshop.'

'You could write competency-based questions that would show you how people cope with emergencies, what sort of books they would want to acquire, and what knowledge they have of storing books appropriately,' said

Jemma. 'Or you could give them an emergency scenario and ask what they would do.'

Raphael picked up his coffee cup and drained it. 'This is much more work than I thought it would be,' he said. 'Why don't you just take the job?'

Jemma goggled at him. 'Don't be ridiculous, Raphael,' she snapped. 'I have no idea how to look after valuable books, I don't know what I'd do in a knowledge-related emergency, and I've spent less than six months working in a bookshop.' She felt heat creep up her neck. 'I'm not qualified, according to your criteria, and apart from anything else, you can't afford me.'

'Oh,' said Raphael. 'Is that your final word on the subject?'

'Yes, it is,' said Jemma. 'I'm surprised at you, Raphael. The system you've got at the moment is why you ended up with someone like Brian working for you. There's no job security, the pay is terrible, and I sincerely doubt that this is a family-friendly job. Frankly, I'm disappointed.' She stood up, and pushed her chair in.

As Jemma turned to go she saw Carl framed in the great oak doorway, staring at her. 'Excuse me,' she said, marching towards him, 'I have a bookshop to run.' And still staring, he got out of her way.

Chapter 4

Jemma arrived back at her own bookshop to find a small note hanging from the knocker. *Stocktake in progress: please knock or ring for admission.* She let herself in and, as ever, was surprised when no bell rang. There was no bell. She imagined Brian's face at being summoned by a bell, like a grocer, or a vendor of something he would consider less classy than books.

'I'm back,' she called, removing her jacket. 'Are you in the stockroom?'

There was no answer, but presently Maddy appeared with not a hair out of place. 'Sorry, I was in the middle of something,' she said. She looked Jemma up and down, taking in her slightly increased smartness. 'You were quick.'

'Yes, it turned out to be recruitment advice, so it didn't take long.'

Maddy's eyes opened a little wider. 'Recruitment advice?'

'That's right,' said Jemma. How much did Maddy know? She couldn't be sure, but she could see that Maddy was interested. 'Seeing as I'm back, would you mind showing me the ropes? Of the stocktaking, I mean.'

Maddy smoothed her hair. 'I, um – yes, of course. Come this way.' She smiled, but it lasted only a moment before it flickered and went out.

Over the next half hour, Jemma was inducted into the mysteries of book care. Maddy showed her the special boxes that the most valuable books were kept in, often made to measure, and the thermostat in the stockroom. 'I always check it when I come in, and when I leave for the day,' she said. 'If it's colder than nineteen degrees or warmer than twenty-one, I take action. And if it's a particularly hot or cold day, I check it at lunchtime as well. It only takes a second, but it's essential for peace of mind.'

'And how do you know where everything is?' asked Jemma.

Maddy laughed. 'Oh, that's easy. Each set of shelves has a letter, and each individual shelf, a number. We arrange books by subject, so botany goes here' – she pointed – 'and art here.' She twisted round and pointed the other way. 'So when we bring in a new book we type its details into the computer, add the shelf code, and that's it. If it has its own box, of course, we label that. There's a label maker under the counter.'

'I see,' said Jemma, gazing about her. Brian's stockroom was perhaps a sixth of the size of Raphael's, if that, and meticulously organised. 'Do you find that the books stay where you put them?'

'I'm not sure what you mean,' said Maddy. 'The shelves are very sturdy, so we've never had any collapses.'

'I'm sure you haven't,' said Jemma. She ran a finger along the nearest shelf when Maddy wasn't looking, and it came away clean. 'I mean, have you ever come in here for a book and found it wasn't where you expected it to be?'

Maddy shook her head. 'No, never. The system is agreed. So long as everyone knows what's going on, nothing should go astray.'

'And you've never… You've never found a book in your stockroom that you didn't expect to be there?'

Maddy's head-shaking became more vigorous. 'We keep track of everything,' she said. 'If we found something unexpected in the stockroom, that would mean it hadn't been catalogued.' She frowned as if this possibility had never occurred to her. Then she gazed at Jemma. 'Would you mind me asking,' she said, 'what the position is that you were advising on?'

'I'm not sure I can,' said Jemma. 'I haven't been sworn to secrecy exactly, but it isn't my job to discuss.'

'So it isn't a job here,' said Maddy.

Jemma smiled. 'No, it isn't,' she said. 'It's nothing to do with me.'

'Oh,' said Maddy. 'I see. Would you like a cup of tea? We're just about finished.'

'Yes, please, if you don't mind,' said Jemma. 'That would be lovely.'

While Maddy was making tea Jemma took the

opportunity to nip upstairs and fetch her laptop cable. *Hmmm,* she thought as she came back downstairs. Maddy was clearly relieved that the recruitment wasn't for their shop. *Perhaps she's worried I'll replace her.* Jemma heaved a sigh. *She really shouldn't be. I wouldn't have the first clue how to run this place.*

But you can run a bookshop, said a surprisingly encouraging inner voice. *You've done it, remember? And Raphael still relies on you.*

That's different, she told it as she opened the door into the bookshop, cable in hand. *I run a general bookshop, not a bookshop like this.*

But you don't want it to be a bookshop like this, the little voice insisted. *You want it to be different. What about that book you read last night? And your plan?*

You be quiet and let me think things over, Jemma told it, as Maddy handed her a mug of tea. The mugs here were all bone china. 'Thank you, Maddy.'

And anyway, the voice piped up, *it should be much easier here, because it doesn't look as if this bookshop is magical. It just does what it's told.*

'You could be right,' said Jemma.

Maddy turned surprised eyes on her. 'Excuse me?'

'I, um, I said that I hope Luke has a good night,' said Jemma. 'You know, Luke who works at the other bookshop. He's going speed dating tonight.'

Maddy looked at her feet. 'Luke's the – the young man in black, isn't he?'

'That's right,' said Jemma. She had once, in a moment of managerial enthusiasm, brought Luke and Carl to say hello to Maddy, hoping that they would get along and perhaps be able to work between the bookshops. The experience had been five minutes of embarrassed shuffling and one-word responses which she never wanted to repeat.

'Oh,' said Maddy. She took the teabag out of her cup of camomile tea and put it neatly in the bin.

'I thought you usually left it in,' said Jemma.

'What?' Maddy followed Jemma's gaze to her mug. 'Oh. I don't like it too strong, though.' She paused. 'Have you considered new acquisitions?'

'I can't say that I have, yet,' said Jemma. 'I mean, I feel as if I've only been here five minutes.'

'Oh yes, I understand that,' said Maddy. 'But with Brian's, um, departure, it's important that people still have a reason to come to the shop. He was known for his select but interesting stock.'

'I gathered,' said Jemma. 'What did he specialise in?' She noted, in passing, that this was the first time Maddy had referred to the fact that Brian was no longer there.

'Rare antiquarian books,' said Maddy. 'For preference, nineteenth century or earlier, and always non-fiction.' She giggled. It was rather an odd sound, as if she wasn't used to doing it. 'He always said that novels were a pack of lies.'

'Did he,' said Jemma. She hadn't thought it possible, but Brian went down another notch in her estimation.

'Yes, he said—' Maddy winced and put a hand to her head. 'Oh dear,' she said. 'I think I have a headache coming on.'

'Why don't you sit quietly for a bit,' said Jemma. 'Do you need to take something?' She looked under the back-room sink for the first-aid kit, but of course it wasn't there. *Definitely not a magical shop*, the little voice muttered.

'No, no, I'm sure I'll be fine in a minute,' said Maddy. 'Perhaps it's dust from the stockroom.'

'I doubt it,' said Jemma. 'It's absolutely spotless in there.'

'I think I need peace and quiet,' said Maddy. She sat down, put her camomile tea on the table, and rested her head in her hands, massaging her temples gently. 'Would you mind switching off the lights?'

'Of course,' said Jemma. 'I'll go through and mind the shop.'

She went through and took the sign off the door, then plugged in her laptop and typed in her password. Immediately her action plan filled the screen, in all its multicoloured glory. Jemma scrolled through it, then sipped her tea and put it out of harm's way. She scrolled left, so that the more ambitious milestones exited stage right. Then she looked at her initial goals.

- *Learn more about the stock.* She pursed her lips and changed the cell colour to light green. There was still work to be done, but she had a much better idea of what she was dealing with.

- *Find out if the shop is magic, and if so, how much.* Jemma selected a neon-bright green for this one, and in the notes column, typed: *Not at all. It's a completely normal bookshop.*

- *Get to know Maddy better and find out what drives her.*

Jemma frowned. From what she had seen, Maddy was devoted to the bookshop. She seemed genuinely relieved to learn that Jemma wasn't planning to recruit new staff for her shop, and she might even have accepted that Brian wasn't coming back. At least, not for another ten years. It was definitely progress of sorts, so Jemma coloured the cell light green.

The cursor winked in the comments field. Jemma thought for a moment, and typed: *Continue to talk to Maddy. Find out what, if anything, she does outside work. Be nice to her.*

I'm never not nice to her, she thought indignantly. Then she remembered her little snipe earlier that morning, and felt herself going pink. *OK, I'll try.*

The door to the back room opened and Maddy stood there, looking rather pale. 'I've had a rest, and I feel much better,' she said, walking into the shop.

It can't be easy for Maddy, Jemma thought. *She's probably worked here for years, and she's used to having things just so. This must all have been a shock. Be kind*, Jemma added in the comments box, then closed the laptop and smiled at her. But Maddy, who almost appeared to be sleepwalking, didn't smile back.

Chapter 5

Jemma was doing the stocktake in the bookshop, but it was taking a lot longer than when Maddy did it. For one thing, several of the books weren't where they were supposed to be. Some weren't even in their protective boxes. And when Maddy checked the thermostat, it was a full two degrees higher than it should have been. 'The books will spoil,' she said, fixing Jemma with a stern eye. 'And that will be your fault. I suggest that you go to bed.'

'What a good idea,' said Jemma. 'I'll see you in the morning, then.'

'Oh no, you can't leave the stockroom,' said Maddy. 'You have to mind the books. Here, I've made up a bed for you.' She pointed to a large wooden box with a blanket in it. 'You'll be fine in there. You fit perfectly, I've checked. So if you'll just climb in, I'll put the lid on—'

'I don't think that's a good idea,' said Jemma, taking a

step back.

'Why's that?' asked Maddy, advancing. 'Don't you like the way we do things in the shop?' Her hand shot out and grabbed Jemma's wrist. 'Come along, you'll like it when you get used to it.' Then somehow Jemma was in the box and trying to get out, but her hands slipped on its smooth sides. Now the lid was closing— 'Help!' she yelled, and thrust upwards with all her strength.

Her eyes opened. It was pitch black, possibly because she had managed to pull the throw she kept on the chesterfield sofa over her face. But when she struggled free, it was still dark outside. Something was digging into her back. She felt around carefully and retrieved *Pigs Have Wings*, which looked slightly the worse for its experience.

Oh dear. She glanced at her phone: a quarter past four. She sighed, padded upstairs to her bedroom, and lay down as she was. After all, she'd have to get up in three hours.

It's been ages since I had a nightmare, she thought, but she didn't bother to interrogate the cause. She knew perfectly well.

Jemma had tried her best to honour her new action point to be kind to Maddy, but somehow, it wasn't bearing the fruit she had hoped for. Far from the glimpses of possible companionship, and a future for the bookshop without Brian in it, Maddy had grown even more set in her ways. When Jemma had suggested gently that perhaps the bookshop could widen its remit and introduce a shelf of classic novels, plays, and poetry, Maddy's head had pulled back and her nostrils had flared, as if she were a warhorse ready to charge.

'I'm not sure what our customers would make of that,' she said, fetching a cloth and wiping an invisible smear from the counter. When a customer came in, she asked him – after she had fulfilled his requirements, of course. 'While you're here, Mr De Vere,' she had said, 'Jemma wonders whether we should present classic fiction in addition to our current offer.'

Mr De Vere, a lean man in a tweed jacket, snorted. 'Not for me, thank you,' he said, regarding Jemma as if she were a slug on his salad. 'The shop is fine as it is. I wouldn't want it – diluted – with fiction.' He leaned forward and murmured something to Maddy which Jemma was too far away to catch.

Maddy considered, and as she did so, Jemma moved closer. The pair of them eyed her, then Maddy said, 'I really couldn't say.'

'Since you're here, Mr De Vere,' said Jemma, feeling that as she was already in his bad books it couldn't hurt to sink any lower, 'are there any other books you might be interested in? I'm thinking of compiling a database of customers' interests.'

Mr De Vere ignored her while he put his purchase into the large leather satchel he had brought for the purpose. Only then did he respond. 'When I want a book, my dear, I shall come in and ask for it. Good day to you.'

'That went well,' said Jemma, once the door had closed behind him.

Maddy turned, and Jemma almost recoiled at her forbidding expression. 'We do not solicit the customers in the shop,' she said.

'Why not?' said Jemma. 'Usually people like being asked what their interests are.'

'Our relationships with our clients go back years,' said Maddy. 'You can't expect to get chummy with them in a matter of days.'

'Then maybe we need friendlier customers,' said Jemma. 'Meanwhile, I need tea.' And she stomped to the back room in high dudgeon.

The rest of the afternoon had been no better. They had two more serious customers who also rejected the idea that the shop might stock even Folio Society editions of appropriate fiction. In between, a sprinkling of browsers were scared off either by the books or by Maddy, who had told one customer with great contempt that they did not stock chick lit.

'If that's what you're looking for,' said Jemma, 'why don't you try Burns Books? It's just down the road that way. They have lots of fiction, including chick lit, and a café.'

'Oh, right,' said the woman, slinging her handbag more firmly over her shoulder. 'Thanks for that, I'll go there now. I could just fancy a coffee.'

Maddy was silent until the customer had left. Then she rounded on Jemma. 'What did you do that for?'

Jemma shrugged. 'If we don't have what she wants, it's only reasonable to send her to a shop that does. Perhaps they'll send people our way, too.'

Maddy muttered something.

'I didn't quite catch that,' said Jemma.

'I said,' Maddy declared, clear as a bell, 'that left up to

you, the shop would be run into the ground within a fortnight. Sending people to our competitors?'

'They aren't our competitors,' said Jemma. 'In case you've forgotten, I work for both shops, and I don't see why they can't complement each other. Perhaps you should stop being so narrow-minded.'

Maddy muttered again at that, and Jemma decided that, whatever she was saying, she couldn't be bothered to listen to it. They had spent the rest of the afternoon in different parts of the shop.

They closed bang on five o'clock, as usual. *So much for kindness*, thought Jemma. She gazed around the beautiful, cold shop, and sighed. Then she texted Carl. *Just finished here. Want to come round? I'll cook.*

It took longer for him to reply than usual. Jemma sat at the shop counter, waiting. It wasn't as if she needed to go anywhere. *Sorry, not tonight. I'm meeting up with Rumpus. Will you be in the shop tomorrow?*

Jemma's eyebrows rose. *I thought rehearsals were yesterday*, she replied.

His response was quicker this time. *They were. This is something else.*

Jemma rolled her eyes. He really wasn't getting the message. *When are you meeting them?* she texted.

7.30, but I've got stuff to do first. Can we talk tomorrow?

~~*No, I want to talk now!*~~

~~*I've had a rotten day and I want someone to be nice to me.*~~

~~*My plan isn't working and I don't know what to do.*~~

Sure, see you tomorrow. Jemma had debated putting a kiss on the end of her message, but decided he didn't deserve it. And now, huddled in a cold bed in the dead of night, she still felt exactly the same.

***

Jemma woke the next morning sticky-eyed and grumpy. Everything still rankled. What annoyed her most was that she had succumbed to the lure of a Snacking Cross Road double-pepperoni pizza and two cans of full-fat Coke. No wonder she hadn't slept well. 'Bad choices, Jemma,' she groaned as she peeled herself out of bed.

At least I don't have to face Maddy this morning, she thought, staring at her doleful reflection in the bathroom mirror.

But you do have to face Raphael.

She winced, and turned the shower on.

Two slices of toast and a strong coffee later, she felt slightly more human. *I suppose I should apologise*, she thought, as she put mascara on.

'Yes, you should,' said a voice rather like her mother's. 'He thinks you're capable. Let's face it, you need people like that.'

Jemma had an almost overriding impulse to put her mascara away and slam the cabinet door on that annoying little voice, but remembered just in time that she had only done one eye. So she endured more nagging, her mouth half-open so that she couldn't even retort, then took great pleasure in shutting it in for the day.

At least once she got to the shop Luke looked his normal, slightly scruffy self. 'How did it go?' she asked.

Luke glanced up from *The Language of Film*. 'Good, thanks,' he said.

'And…?' she prompted.

The book lowered. 'I'm going on a date tonight,' he said. 'Drinks, then a movie. I'm finishing early so that I can get ready.'

'Oh, right,' said Jemma. 'Hope it goes well.'

'Raphael isn't in yet,' said Luke. 'Carl is setting up.'

Jemma checked her watch. 'He's early,' she said.

'Yeah, he's finishing a bit early tonight too,' said Luke. 'Something about a project.'

Everyone but me's got stuff going on, thought Jemma, pushing her hair out of her eyes. But she merely said 'Uh-huh,' and headed downstairs.

She heard whistling as she pushed open the oak door. Carl was sweeping the floor. 'Oh, hi,' he said, leaning on his broom.

'Hi,' said Jemma. 'Have you got time for a cappuccino?'

He hesitated. 'Yeah, go on then. The machine's on.'

Jemma sat at one of the café tables and watched him make her drink. 'Luke says you've got a project on,' she said, as he sprinkled cocoa powder on top.

His shoulders stiffened a fraction. Then he picked up the cup and brought it over. 'Here you go,' he said. Then he took a seat opposite her. 'I've been working on something.'

'With Rumpus? Is that what yesterday's meeting was about?'

Carl smiled. 'Yeah.' He leaned back in his chair. 'That

night we didn't go out, I had an idea for a play. And I had a go at writing it.'

'Oh.' Jemma stared at him. 'But you don't—'

'I know,' said Carl. 'It was weird. I got some paper, I thought about the characters, a line came into my head, and I wrote it down. The rest just sort of happened. I wasn't going to say anything, but then I mentioned to Josie that I'd written a play. She made me tell her about it, then said I should tell everyone. So I did, and last night we did a read-through. And they want to do it.'

'Do it?' Jemma echoed. 'You mean—'

'Put it on. I mean, it needs work, I know it needs work, but we could workshop it and then maybe ask Raphael. It's set in a bookshop, you see.' He grinned. 'Write what you know, and all that.'

'Wow,' said Jemma. 'That's great. No, that's brilliant. It really is. I'm so pleased for you.' She reached out and squeezed his hand, but the gesture felt inadequate.

'Thanks,' said Carl. 'How did your plan go?'

Jemma drank her cappuccino while she considered her answer. There was so much she wanted to tell him, and she sensed that pouring her heart out would get the poison out of her system. But she couldn't do it. She couldn't dump that negativity on him, not when he was doing such a cool new thing. 'Early days,' she said. 'I'm working on things.' She took a deep draught of her coffee. 'Anyway, I'd better leave you to it if you've got things to do.' She got up.

Carl studied her. 'OK,' he said, eventually. Then he got up, took her cup, and slotted it into the dishwasher. 'Maybe see you later?'

Jemma forced a smile. 'Sure,' she said. 'See you later.'

She walked slowly back upstairs, undecided whether she would be more miserable in Carl's company or Luke's. *If ever there was a day not to be around people…* 'I'm just nipping into the stockroom,' she called to Luke. 'Let me know when Raphael comes down.'

She switched the light on and wandered along the aisles, looking at the rows of book-filled boxes and seeing nothing. *Of course Maddy would have a label maker*, she thought sourly. Then she stopped, turned to a shelf, and rested her forehead on the nearest box. *What am I going to do? I have no authority in my own shop. My. Own. Shop.*

'Then take it,' whispered a little voice.

Jemma jumped, and stared at the box as if it had spoken to her. 'How?'

'Maddy sees you as an inferior,' the whisper came, a little louder this time. 'But if you were Assistant Keeper…'

'But what if I don't want to be Assistant Keeper?' Jemma rubbed her forehead. *I'm talking to a box. This is ridiculous.*

'But I'm giving you answers,' the little voice said. 'Think about it. It doesn't have to be for ever.'

Possibilities swam in Jemma's mind. If she were busy learning Assistant Keeper duties, no one could expect her to make sweeping changes in the bookshop. With that added authority, she would feel more able to give orders to Maddy. And as it was only temporary, then assuming no major disasters occurred, no one could blame her if she didn't get things exactly right.

A gentle tap at the door. 'Anyone home?' called Raphael.

'Sshh,' Jemma told the box, then clapped her hand over her mouth. 'I'm in here,' she said. 'Have you got new stock in?'

Raphael entered, resplendent in a maroon velvet smoking jacket, teal-coloured trousers, and a pale-grey shirt with a teal silk cravat. 'Yes, I have,' he said. 'I've been thinking, and perhaps you are right.'

'I've been thinking too,' said Jemma, 'and I agree. I wouldn't be suited to the permanent job, but if you like, I could take it on while you recruit somebody. So long as you teach me the basics.'

'Oh,' said Raphael. He studied her for perhaps a minute. 'I hadn't expected that. You were rather—'

'I've slept on it,' said Jemma, 'and I need a challenge.'

'Well,' said Raphael, 'if we're recruiting in the, er, approved manner, it would help to have somebody holding the fort in the meantime.'

'Good,' said Jemma. 'So that's settled, then.' She walked towards Raphael and stuck out a hand. 'Pleasure to work with you, boss,' she said, plastering a wide, confident smile on her face. And as Raphael, looking bewildered, shook it, she wished with all her heart that she felt even a tenth as confident beneath.

Chapter 6

'As luck would have it,' said Raphael, 'we are in exactly the right place to begin.' He swept a hand round the stockroom.

Jemma swallowed. She hadn't expected her instruction to commence quite so soon. 'W – where is the thermostat?' she asked.

Raphael's hand was arrested mid-gesture. 'The which?'

'The thermostat,' said Jemma. 'To keep the books at the right temperature.'

Comprehension dawned. 'Oh,' said Raphael. 'You've been listening to Maddy, haven't you?' He smiled. 'The shop does that.'

'Is that why our books aren't in special boxes?' said Jemma.

'Exactly. The stockroom preserves the books for me.'

'But how does it know?' asked Jemma.

They heard a meow outside the door. Raphael raised an eyebrow. 'I suspect Folio wishes to be involved.' He opened the door and let the cat in. Folio strolled towards the table and chair which Luke used, jumped on the chair, and sat watching them.

'In answer to your question,' said Raphael, 'the shop is enchanted. Various powerful charms protect any book that comes in here. Allow me to demonstrate.' He reached for the nearest box and took out a book. 'This is one of my favourites,' he said. 'It's a book of cures, lotions and poultices, compiled by a woman called Sukey Nobbs in the fifteenth century. There is more practical wisdom in this than in many a modern textbook. Jemma, could you go to the far end of that aisle, pull out any box, and take out the first book you find.'

Jemma did as she was told. '*On Life and Death*,' she read. '*Essays.*'

'That'll do nicely,' said Raphael. He took two steps forward. 'Now walk towards me. Oh, and hold the book out.'

Jemma did as she was told, feeling exceptionally silly. 'I really don't understand what this is—'

She stopped, not of her own volition. She felt as if she had walked into an invisible wall.

'That's it,' said Raphael. 'Have another go.'

Jemma's foot moved forward, then stopped. She tried to hold the book out, but her arm just wouldn't stretch.

'As you can see, we have a slight problem,' said Raphael. 'However, it is easily solved. I want you to tell the book that you are an Assistant Keeper.'

Jemma looked at the book, then at Raphael, and shrugged. 'I'm an assistant keeper,' she mumbled.

'Not like that,' said Raphael. 'As if you believe it. Come on, stand tall.'

Jemma stared at him. 'Is this necessary?'

'Oh, absolutely,' said Raphael. 'Come on, have a try.'

Jemma took a deep breath. 'I am an Assistant Keeper,' she said, louder.

The book vibrated in her hand.

'That's better,' said Raphael. 'Once more. Imagine you want Maddy to hear you.'

That did it. Jemma filled her lungs and shouted 'I am an Assistant Keeper!'

'There,' said Raphael. 'Try moving now.'

Jemma took a step forward, then another, until she was perhaps two feet away from Raphael. 'That will do,' he said.

'It works,' said Jemma. 'It really works.' She gazed at the book in her hand, which resonated with a gentle hum. Then she peered closer. 'Is it glowing?'

'It is,' said Raphael. 'Probably best that you take a step back. No point in wasting the power. Now you can see why I keep books like these well apart.'

'So do you actually know where all the important books are in the stockroom?' asked Jemma. This was a level of organisation she would never have suspected of Raphael.

'Not as such,' Raphael replied. 'I tend to assume that this room, given the enchantments it has, will keep things apart that need to be kept apart.'

'But how does that work in – in *my* shop?' asked Jemma. 'It isn't magical.'

'Don't be too sure,' said Raphael. 'It may not be as magical as this shop, but few places are.'

'But if it were,' said Jemma, 'then why would it need the thermostat, and the special boxes, and the cataloguing system?'

'Maybe it does need some of those things,' said Raphael. 'Or maybe that's just smoke and mirrors to keep Maddy happy. Who knows?' He smiled. 'What you *could* do is look for the more – interesting – resources, and see if you can bring them together. If you can do that without telling the books that you're an Assistant Keeper, then yes, it probably is a normal shop.' He sighed. 'I do hope for your sake that it isn't, Jemma. That would be remarkably dull.'

'So should I assume that everything is stored correctly?' said Jemma.

'Have there been any fires?' asked Raphael.

'Of course not,' said Jemma. 'What do you take me for?'

'Floods? Plagues of insects? Things or people disappearing?'

Jemma shook her head.

'In that case,' said Raphael, 'you're probably fine. But maybe check, to be on the safe side.'

'How did you learn all this?' asked Jemma.

'I spent a lot of time in my uncle's bookshop when I was a boy,' said Raphael. 'He taught me to read. I don't remember him telling me anything, as such, but I sort of absorbed it.'

'Is he still alive?' asked Jemma, wide-eyed.

'Good heavens, no,' said Raphael. 'Unfortunately the plague got him.'

'The – the Great Plague?' asked Jemma.

'That's the one,' said Raphael. 'And then the fire finished off the bookshop. Not a great decade, I think you'll agree.'

'No,' said Jemma, faintly. 'I don't suppose it was.' She felt her mind reaching for something to grasp hold of, something that made sense. 'So if there is an incident,' she said, 'what should I do?'

'If books are too close together,' said Raphael, 'the best thing to do is to move them apart, taking care that in doing so you don't move them towards another book they might react with.'

'OK,' said Jemma. 'Move books apart, keeping clear of other books.'

'If a book is damaged, then in the first instance bring it to me for inspection,' said Raphael. 'Obviously, in this shop we have some stock which is in, shall we say, not the best condition. But if it's a standard volume, carefully applied sticky tape will probably do the trick.'

'And if it isn't?' Jemma imagined torn parchment, accidentally dogeared pages, cracked spines. Now she understood the reason for all that glass.

'Bring it to me,' said Raphael, 'and we shall decide what is best to do given the age, value, and importance of the item.' He paused, considering. 'Your shop's stock is different from mine. You have far fewer books, but on average they are more valuable.' He grinned. 'I have to admit I was rather impressed when he brought out Archimedes' Palimpsest. I wasn't expecting that.'

'But wouldn't he have had to clear that with you first?' asked Jemma. 'You said in the job description—'

'Ah, but when it's for a challenge,' said Raphael, 'all bets are off. Anything goes, pretty much.' He frowned. 'I should probably have a chat with its previous owners, and find out what he gave them in exchange.'

Folio jumped down from his chair and wound himself round Jemma's legs. Jemma bent to stroke him, then remembered the book in her hand. 'Is it all right to—' She mimed stroking.

'Oh yes, of course,' said Raphael. 'Folio is very much attuned to the books. He won't damage them.'

'Good,' said Jemma, crouching and giving him a proper fuss. 'With everything else going on, I need to be able to stroke my favourite cat.' Folio let out an extremely loud purr.

'Mmm,' said Raphael. 'What else is going on?'

Drat, thought Jemma. 'I meant with Luke dating,' she said, 'and Carl's play.'

'And...?' Raphael's blue eyes were sympathetic, but Jemma felt them boring into her.

She sighed. 'I'm having a hard time with Maddy,' she said. 'She's resistant to change. Of any kind. Even adding fiction to the stock. And the customers share her views.'

'That must be frustrating,' said Raphael.

'Just slightly,' said Jemma. She looked around the stockroom and sighed again. 'What was the shop like when you took it on?'

'Sparse,' said Raphael. 'Specialist. A collector's shop.'

'So you've been through this too!' cried Jemma. 'What did you do?'

'Well,' said Raphael, 'as I won with a combination of three printed books, I decided that print was the way to go, and the more modern the better. It took until the late nineteenth century to pay off, though. Admittedly one of my printed books was Shakespeare's First Folio, but it's all relative.'

Jemma looked at the cat. 'Is that where Folio got his name?'

Folio sauntered over to Raphael and gazed at him expectantly. Raphael pulled a packet of cat treats from his pocket and gave him a couple. 'That's right,' he said, 'although I got Folio slightly before I took on the shop.'

'So he's immortal too?' Jemma gazed at Folio, who narrowed his eyes and gave her a sharp meow.

'Not immortal,' said Raphael. 'Neither of us are. Just – lucky. And certain, um, protections come with the job.'

'Oh,' said Jemma. She thought for a moment. 'Does that apply to all these sorts of jobs?'

'Not to the same degree,' said Raphael. 'But yes.'

'So if I took the job, permanently,' Jemma said slowly, 'I wouldn't die?'

'Not unless there was a major major incident,' said Raphael. 'You wouldn't get any older, either.'

Jemma had a sudden vision of Carl in thirty years' time: maybe grey-haired, maybe balding, and herself looking just the same. 'Oh,' she said.

'Indeed,' said Raphael. 'It's a blessing, and a curse. It's – difficult to form relationships with outsiders, since you know they won't be around for long. Comparatively speaking.'

'Oh dear,' said Jemma. Suddenly she felt more sorry for the ageless, powerful man in front of her than she would ever have thought possible. 'That doesn't apply to temporary staff, does it?'

Raphael laughed. 'No, Jemma, you're quite safe. Though some people see it as a perk.'

Jemma remembered the Assistant Curator at Sir John Soane's Museum, and wondered.

'That's enough for now,' Raphael said gently. 'You've taken in a lot of information, and I don't want to overload you on your first day. Let's go downstairs and get a drink, and you can help me finish the job description. If we're doing this thing, we should get on with it. Then you can head over to your shop and check your own assets.'

'Yes,' said Jemma, dreamily. 'Yes, I can. I can check the assets in my shop.' She smiled. 'Come on then,' she said, 'I could murder a brew.'

They tidied the stockroom, let Folio out, then left. Jemma popped her head into the main shop, where Luke was buried in his book. 'Sorry about the noise,' she said.

Luke looked up. 'What noise?'

'You know,' said Jemma. 'The shouting.'

Luke considered this, then shrugged. 'Didn't hear anything.'

Jemma scrutinised as much of him as she could see, but he didn't appear to be making fun of her. Reflecting that the day couldn't get much stranger, she walked downstairs to join Raphael. 'I am an Assistant Keeper,' she whispered, very quietly, and felt the thrum of thousands of books, listening.

Chapter 7

Jemma returned to her shop armed with new knowledge and a cheese and Parma ham panini. When she reached it, she stepped back and surveyed it critically. *Would I want to shop in here?*

The answer was a resounding no.

Why, exactly?

The bookshop looks boring, she thought. *All that black paintwork. I don't like the name; all it tells me is that someone with the initials BJF sells old books. I don't know if they're interesting, just old. And as there's only one book in the window and I can't see what it's called, there's no way for me to tell if I'd like it or not.*

Well, I can't do anything about the name of the shop or the paintwork just yet. But I can deal with that display.

She opened the silent door. Maddy, as usual, was alone. 'Hi, Maddy,' she called. 'Busy morning?' She kept her face neutral as she said it.

Maddy glanced up from an auction catalogue. 'Nice and quiet, thank you. Just two customers, and we had what they wanted.'

'I've been thinking,' said Jemma. 'I'd like to encourage more customers into the shop.'

Maddy opened her mouth to reply, but Jemma held up a hand. 'Please let me finish. I know you don't want to broaden the bookshop's stock and our existing customers don't either, but I can't help thinking that if we put affordable books in the window, it might encourage more people in to buy what we already have. With a greater range of customers, we may find that they have different needs.'

Maddy sniffed. 'The bookshop does make a profit,' she said.

'Based on a few customers who have the money to buy our more expensive items,' said Jemma. 'If we lost even one or two of those customers we'd feel it, wouldn't we?'

Maddy said nothing.

'So what I would like you to do, Maddy,' said Jemma, 'is go through our stock and find me eight or nine attractive books priced at less than fifty pounds. Preferably less than twenty-five. How much is that book in the window?'

Maddy told her.

'Better make that nine,' said Jemma. 'It's not surprising that people don't come in. Now, have you had your lunch? If you'd like to go out, I can eat mine here.'

'I haven't,' said Maddy. 'And yes, I think I will go out today.' She closed the auction catalogue, picked up her hessian shopper, and slipped it inside. She did this without looking at Jemma. 'Bye,' she muttered, and made for the door.

Jemma sat in Maddy's still-warm seat. She was halfway through her panini and a re-read of Appendix 2 of *Your Business, Your Way* when a cough alerted her to the presence of a customer.

She swallowed her mouthful hurriedly. 'I'm terribly sorry, I didn't hear you come in,' she said. *I'm getting a bell put on that door,* she thought. *I don't care whether Brian would approve.*

The customer, a woman with expensive blonde highlights, wearing something tailored and obviously designer, raised an eyebrow. 'Is Brian in, please?'

Jemma considered how to answer. 'He doesn't work here at present,' she said.

'Maddy, then.'

'She's on her lunch break,' said Jemma, 'so I'm afraid you'll have to make do with me.' She stood up and extended a hand. 'I'm Jemma, the new manager of the shop.'

The woman looked at the hand. 'Are you,' she said. 'In that case, I want an early edition of Darwin's *Origin of Species*. First edition and original binding if possible, but I don't mind so long as it is in excellent condition. It's a present.'

'I'll check our database,' said Jemma. She moved to the computer and typed in search terms. 'We have one first edition in reasonable condition, and a fourth edition described as being "as new". Would you like to see them both?'

The woman studied Jemma as if she were a talking dog. 'Um, yes please,' she said.

The fourth edition was shelved in the main shop, while the other was in the stockroom. 'I shouldn't be long,' said Jemma, hoping fervently that she wouldn't. *B7*, she repeated in her head as she scanned the shelves.

The book was exactly where it should be, in a labelled case. Jemma felt a rush of unexpected warmth towards Maddy. 'Thank you,' she whispered, and picked up the case. She laid it on the counter, then unlocked a glass door in the main shop and brought out the second book. Both were green, both had gilt decoration on the spine. 'Here we are,' she said. 'There's quite a difference in price—'

The woman flapped an impatient hand. 'That one,' she said, pointing at the fourth edition. 'I'd prefer the other, but there isn't time to get it restored.' She sighed. 'These last-minute birthday invitations are so tiresome.'

'I'm sure whoever receives it will love it,' said Jemma. 'It's a very generous gift.'

The woman smiled for the first time since she had entered the shop. Her teeth were white and even, and there was a tiny gap between each. 'It's a convenient gift,' she said. She opened her bag, extracted a small purse, and took out a plain black card.

'Well, if you need any more last-minute book presents,' said Jemma, 'you know where we are.' She took payment and handed over the receipt. 'Would you like a bag?'

The customer considered. 'It's probably best,' she concluded. 'Excuse me a moment.' She went to the door, beckoned, and presently a uniformed man came in and bore the book away. 'Thank you, er—'

'Jemma,' said Jemma.

The woman seemed to be considering whether that could possibly be her name. Eventually, she nodded. 'Thank you, Jemma.' And she sailed out.

As soon as the door closed, Jemma slumped on the counter with a huge sigh of relief. Then she started laughing. *I made a sale! I made a sale, on my own, and nothing bad happened!* It was only when she straightened up that she realised her half-eaten panini had been sitting next to her on the counter all along.

***

'Quiet, I suppose,' said Maddy, when she returned.

'Just one customer,' said Jemma. She had considered whether to swap her business book for *Pigs Have Wings* before Maddy got back, but decided that what she chose to read was up to her.

Maddy hung up her jacket and bag, and removed the auction catalogue. 'Will you be going out?'

'No thanks, I'm fine,' said Jemma. 'Oh yes, and we have a gap on that shelf.' She pointed to the empty space where *Origin of Species* had been.

Maddy gaped. 'You sold one?'

'I did,' said Jemma, trying not to puff up. 'For the price listed on the database. And I've updated the record.'

'Oh,' said Maddy, still gazing at the empty space. 'Um, good.'

'Actually,' said Jemma, 'why don't you make yourself a drink, then look for cheaper stock for the window? Maybe pick out fifteen to twenty books, so we can choose the ones that complement each other for the display.' She beamed at Maddy, then returned to her book.

'Would you – would you like a drink too?' asked Maddy. Her voice was slightly thick and hoarse, as if she were having trouble forming the words.

'Oh, yes please,' said Jemma. 'Tea with milk and one sugar, if you would.'

Maddy said no more, but went into the back room. Jemma noted that her usually beautiful posture was slightly off; her upper back curved, her shoulders slightly forward, her head down. She bit her lip. *Am I being mean?*

Give over, said a little voice which Jemma thought of as coming from the book. *You're setting the direction for your business. It's a perfectly normal request. And you asked nicely.*

I did, didn't I? thought Jemma. *And I'm including her in the choosing process, so I'm empowering her.* Feeling almost unbearably smug, she returned to her book.

'It's no good,' said Maddy, ten minutes later. 'Only six books in the shop cost less than fifty pounds, and three of those are in poor condition.'

Jemma sighed. 'Then we should review our stock,' she said. 'I don't want the shop to be a place for rich people only.'

Maddy shot a glance at her. 'But if that's what the books cost…'

'I'm not saying that we can't sell expensive books,' said Jemma. 'But we should sell affordable ones, too. I mean, could you afford to buy most of the books we sell?'

'Well, no,' said Maddy, 'but that isn't the point—'

'What do you like to read?' Jemma asked.

Maddy recoiled as if she had asked a very personal question. 'I read – I read auction catalogues, and the *Bookseller*, and the *Bookseller's Companion*, of course—'

'I asked you what you *like* to read,' said Jemma. 'I like reading novels, usually contemporary ones with a bit of humour, but I'll try most things.' She went to her bag, pulled out *Pigs Have Wings*, and held it up.

Maddy stared at the book in Jemma's hand. 'I—' She swallowed. 'I like Gothic fiction,' she said. 'Classic Gothic fiction, like Ann Radcliffe.' She looked as if she were confessing a secret shame.

'Like *The Mysteries of Udolpho*?' said Jemma. 'I've seen that in Burns Books, but I don't know what else she wrote.'

'She wrote six novels,' said Maddy, 'but they're hard to get hold of. Some of them—' She paused as if what she were about to say might shock Jemma. 'They're only available *online*.'

'Oh yes, I've got a reading app on my phone,' said Jemma. 'It's great for holidays, but I do prefer a paperback.' She grinned. 'I'm probably Brian's most un-ideal reader.'

A small smile lifted the corner of Maddy's mouth. She leaned forward. 'He doesn't know about the novels,' she whispered. 'I've never told him. But I do like reading auction catalogues,' she said in her normal voice. 'Very interesting.'

'Like reading store catalogues when you were a kid,

and picking out the things you wanted?' said Jemma.

Maddy giggled. 'Kind of.'

'Right,' said Jemma, 'what we'll do is put any cheap books in good condition in the window, and add some between fifty and a hundred pounds. Popular names that people recognise, not obscure stuff. The customer who came in earlier wanted *Origin of Species* for a birthday present, which goes to show. With the money from the sale, what I propose to do is buy good-quality cheaper stock. Agreed?'

'Agreed,' said Maddy. And while Jemma wasn't entirely sure how she had got Maddy on her side, or how on earth she would acquire the new stock that she had spoken of so lightly, she was still pleased with the outcome. *It's remarkable what a bit of confidence can do*, she thought, as Maddy arranged a rainbow of books in the window.

Chapter 8

Jemma monitored customer numbers for the next few days. More people were coming in, certainly, and they were making more sales; but she couldn't be sure that her new strategy was paying off.

The new customers were a little less certain of what they wanted, and more inclined to chat. She could see that Maddy found this unnerving, and looked to her for help. Which was fine, because the regular customers made a beeline for Maddy, and to be honest, Jemma preferred it that way.

One morning Jemma took a tour around the bookshop. There were gaps, undeniable gaps.

'We have a problem,' she said to Maddy.

Maddy's eyes opened wide. 'What sort of problem?'

Jemma grinned. 'We need more books! It's a good problem, Maddy. Only I'm not sure how to go about getting more stock.'

Maddy, eyebrows raised, pointed at the little stack of auction catalogues on the counter.

'We've got more than enough of that sort of thing,' said Jemma. 'We need entry-level books.' She thought for a moment. 'You know what, I'll ask Raphael.' She picked up the phone, and dialled.

Luke answered. 'Hello, Burns Books.'

'Hi Luke, it's Jemma. Is Raphael around? Or could you pass on a message?'

'He's in,' said Luke. 'Hang on a minute, and I'll transfer the call.' His voice was replaced by hold music; for some reason it reminded Jemma of skeletons waltzing in a ballroom.

A few seconds later Jemma heard fumbling, and a cautious 'Hello?'

'Hi, Raphael, it's Jemma. Can I ask you about stock?'

'Um, yes, I suppose you may,' said Raphael. 'What do you want to know?'

Jemma frowned. 'Are you all right? You sound a bit – I don't know, a bit down.'

'I thought you wanted to talk about stock, not psychoanalyse me,' Raphael said tersely.

'OK, well can I come over?'

A pause. 'I'm not sure it's a good time.'

'Why, is the shop busy?'

Silence.

'I'll see you in five minutes, then,' said Jemma, and put the phone down before he could object. Something was clearly not right with Raphael, and while her desire to learn more about the mysteries of acquiring stock was keen, her desire to know exactly what was going on was keener.

***

'It may have begun with the job description.' Raphael dropped a lump of sugar in his coffee and stirred it, then looked sadly at the Danish pastry glistening on its white plate. 'But I can't be sure.'

They were in Rolando's. That in itself worried Jemma. She had had several bookshop-related conversations with Raphael, but never in Rolando's. They had always managed with careful substitutions of words, or even mouthing them when necessary. So as this was an outside-the-bookshop conversation, it must concern a matter more serious than they had ever discussed.

'What began with the job description?' Jemma sipped the Americano she had decided she would need, and put her cup down.

'The dissent,' said Raphael. 'I let it be known that I was considering handling recruitment a different way, and apparently people aren't happy.'

'Why not?' said Jemma. 'I thought it was pretty robust.'

Of course you did, you fool, said her ever-present inner voice. *You wrote a lot of it.*

'I'm sure it is,' said Raphael, 'but having a job description at all was a bone of contention. And while the job itself hasn't changed, your idea of making provision for ousted Keepers annoyed several people.'

'Oh,' said Jemma. That had been the bit she was proudest of. 'Your current system is merciless,' she had told Raphael, her eyes flashing. 'At any time someone could find themselves out of a job and forced to leave their home, since they're banished. What happens if they have kids? What are they supposed to do then, move them to a new school? Get themselves a flat in the adjoining region? And what if they're caring for an elderly relative?' She paused briefly for breath. 'It's an equal opportunities nightmare, Raphael.'

'I thought you might say that,' Raphael had remarked, faintly. 'All right then, tell me what you'd do.'

So Jemma had. To a reasonable extent, it had been included. Banishment would not be complete, but confined to running a similar business or occupying a similar post in the same borough. Moreover, efforts would be made to slot a displaced Keeper into a similar post nearby whenever appropriate. 'So why didn't they like that?' she demanded. 'Less upheaval, and at least it offers some security.'

'As it turns out,' said Raphael, 'everyone who expressed an opinion said they were perfectly happy with things just the way they are.'

'Because it's self-selecting,' said Jemma. 'Only the sort of people who are comfortable with those conditions will apply for those jobs.' In a huff of indignation she looked across at him, and softened immediately. 'I'm sorry,' she said. 'What did they say?'

'Oh, there was grumbling about this being the thin end of the wedge, and that I was likely to get applications from all sorts of people wanting an easy ride.' He grimaced. 'That isn't what bothers me, though. It's the whispers. Nothing direct, of course, but lots of little messages from colleagues of mine, saying they've heard on the grapevine that people are saying I've lost my edge. That I'm softening. Even that my recent victory over Brian was a fluke, and technically ought not to have been allowed.'

'Rubbish,' said Jemma.

'Oh, I'm sorry,' snapped Raphael. 'I forgot how experienced you are in these matters.' Then it was his turn to look guilty. 'I apologise, Jemma. I wasn't expecting such a backlash, and it has shaken me rather. Usually when one wins a challenge it enhances one's reputation and standing, but this time, apparently not.'

'Why do you think that is?' asked Jemma. 'What's different?'

'It's hard to say.' Raphael sipped his coffee, and thought. 'It's been a while since anyone challenged me. Perhaps the fact that Brian dared to do so has made more people consider the possibility. And it has to be said that the books I won with were pretty unconventional.'

'But isn't that a strength?' said Jemma.

'In some ways,' said Raphael. 'But your challenges and the books you chose go on record, so in a sense I showed my hand. Some people, seeing what I chose, may think that's the best I've got. It was, to defeat Brian, but the books have to suit the challenger, and also the circumstances.'

'So you're safe, then,' said Jemma.

'One is never safe in this job,' Raphael replied. 'Someone could walk through the door of the bookshop and challenge me this afternoon, and someone else tomorrow morning, and again the morning after, and I would have to step up every single time.' He sighed. 'I'm not as young as I once was.'

'But if you never get any older—'

'That doesn't mean you don't get tired,' said Raphael. He looked up as a coffee jug refilled his cup. Giulia put a hand on his shoulder, and muttered something in his ear that made him smile. Then she bustled off.

Jemma shifted in her seat. 'I don't like hearing you talk like this,' she said. 'It worries me.'

'I can't say it's my favourite topic of conversation, either,' said Raphael. 'Anyway, you wanted to talk about stock.'

Jemma studied him. 'I do,' she said. 'But if I can help in any way—'

'I'll think about it,' said Raphael. 'Thank you. It's nice to talk to someone who understands. I mean, I'm sure many of my Assistant Keepers would, but there's always that niggling feeling that they might use that knowledge against me.'

Jemma shivered at the thought of an army of subordinates gunning for him. 'I don't know how you can bear it,' she said.

'Mostly, I put it aside,' said Raphael. 'Besides, I'm a wily old fox, and I do find that it helps to be a bumbling idiot.'

'You mean pretend to be a bumbling idiot,' said Jemma.

'Oh no,' said Raphael. 'I really am. Just not in everything.' He took a large bite of his danish pastry, and apart from appreciative noises, was silent for a good minute. 'So, stock,' he said, eventually. 'We *are* going to talk about this.'

Jemma grinned. 'Yes, we are. We're starting to sell more lower-price books, but the catch is that we don't have many left. So I'm after good-quality books that won't break the bank. If possible' – she leaned forward – 'I'd like to get fiction in there.'

'Oooh,' said Raphael. 'So what do you need to know?'

'Firstly,' said Jemma, 'do you have any stock like that which we could put into the shop? Most of your customers want paperbacks. If you had any nice hardbacks, though...'

'I take your point,' said Raphael. 'Although this will probably mean making an arrangement about inventory—'

'Such language, Raphael,' said Jemma reprovingly. 'When I'm looking to strengthen both our respective niches, too.'

'Oh well,' said Raphael, 'if you're strengthening our niches...' He grinned back at her. 'Come and pull a couple of boxes out of the stockroom, and we'll see what turns up. You may have them on a sale-or-return basis.'

'Thank you,' said Jemma. 'But I can't pinch your stock all the time. I need to buy books myself, and I haven't a clue where to begin.'

'Oh, I can talk you through that,' said Raphael. 'But take a couple of boxes from me for now, and see how you get on. Time enough to think about your own book-buying expeditions when you've seen if you can make this *expanded niche* work.' He sipped his coffee. 'Ugh. I need to wash my mouth out.'

A brief foray into the stockroom yielded three boxes of

books. Among the spoils were hardback sets of Jane Austen, Thackeray, and Henry Fielding, a complete Wordsworth, a beautiful edition of *London Labour and the London Poor*, and a book of Aubrey Beardsley drawings which made Jemma blush. The stockroom also yielded rather a dusty Folio, who jumped on the counter and shook himself, releasing a fine mist of particles which made Jemma sneeze. 'What have you been doing?' she asked him.

Folio gazed steadily at her, his eyes golden with a tiny black pupil slit. 'Meow,' he offered.

'Silly cat,' she told him, and concentrated on loading her boxes onto a small wheeled trolley, to transport them to her own shop. But once she had thanked Raphael and left, a fine dust of concern settled on her too. What would happen if Raphael were challenged again, and this time he didn't win? Would he lose both shops? And what would happen to him?

Never mind him, a little voice nagged. *What about you?*

Never mind me, Jemma told it crossly. *I'll be fine. What about Raphael?* And the seeds of that particular worry were far harder to remove than dust from a cat's fur.

Chapter 9

Jemma towed the trolley of books carefully behind her, making sure to keep it level and avoid any bumps in the pavement. She stopped dead when she got to the door of her shop. The trolley, due to momentum, bumped into her hip, and Jemma bit back a swearword.

The swearword wasn't entirely for the trolley.

In the window of BJF Antiquarian Books, the rainbow of books had gone. One book, one expensive-looking book, was spotlighted.

Jemma blinked, then looked again. *After all I said… I thought Maddy was finally on board, and the minute I leave the shop—*

She rattled up to the door and pushed it open, fully on the warpath. But inside, Maddy was laughing with Mr De Vere, and a large leather-bound book hunkered smugly on the counter in its protective box.

'I'm back,' she announced to nobody, and squeaked her way into the stockroom. Once there, she parked the little trolley against the wall and stared at the boxes of books morosely.

There's no point even unpacking them, she thought. *I can't get to the computer, so I can't put them on the system, so I don't know where to shelve them.* Instead, she went and made herself a cup of tea. *The minute he's gone–*

But as Mr De Vere was leaving, another customer greeted Maddy like an old friend. Jemma seethed until she wondered whether she might actually whistle like an old kettle, to let off steam.

Eventually the customer left – without buying, Jemma noted – and she stormed back into the shop. 'Why did you change the display?' she demanded, pointing at the book in the window as if it were the lone contender in an identity parade.

Maddy drew herself up and her lips tightened. 'It was a business decision.'

'What do you mean, business decision? I make the business decisions. I'm in charge of the shop.'

Maddy stood firm. 'I reviewed our sales,' she said. 'We've sold more books since your display went up, but unfortunately, as they're low in value, we've made half what we usually would. Within half an hour of me changing it back we've had two sales. Two *good* sales.'

'Right,' said Jemma, 'show me.' But when Maddy did, she had to admit that the figures were right. If anything, Maddy had been generous in saying that the shop had made half as much.

Oops, said her inner voice. *Maybe that change of direction wasn't such a good idea.*

'I'm still not happy about this,' Jemma said, eyeing Maddy. 'It's been less than a week. You haven't given people time to get used to the change.'

'Mmm,' said Maddy, straightening the card reader on the counter.

'You had no right to do that without asking,' Jemma chided. 'I've a good mind to put that display back exactly as it was.'

Maddy gave the tiniest shrug. 'Unfortunately, you weren't here to ask,' she said. 'You're the boss. But I wouldn't advise it.'

Jemma spent the rest of the day in a fairly even split between annoyance, indecision and resentment towards Maddy for being right. Every so often she glanced at the window, and the sight of the book, lit up as if it had won an award, made her hackles rise.

Mid-afternoon, as an act of mutiny against the shop, she brought her new acquisitions through and put them on the database. But there was no place for fiction in the shop, and no category for it in the database. In the end, Jemma entered them under Z9, an empty shelf in the far corner of the stockroom, to give them a home of sorts. *I ought to fight*, she thought, *but I haven't the energy. I'm worried about Raphael, and sad that I was wrong about the shop, and I honestly don't know if I'm doing harm or good.* So she packed the books away out of sight, closed the stockroom door on them, and got *Pigs Have Wings* out of her bag.

Maddy sold two more books that afternoon, and every time the shop door opened Jemma's heart sank a little lower, as her folly was driven further home. *I really don't know what I'm doing; I'm completely out of my depth. I may as well let Maddy get on with it, because I'm worse than useless.* She studied the clock, willing the hands to move faster and get Maddy out of the shop so that she could mourn her great mistaken idea in peace.

She didn't even look up when Maddy said hello to somebody. Then the person replied, and she almost pulled a muscle as her head shot up.

Carl stood there, an odd expression on his face. 'Hi, Jemma,' he said.

'Um, hi,' said Jemma. *Why is he here?* She couldn't quite take him in.

'I wondered if you fancied going for a quick drink,' he said. 'I can wait while you close the shop.'

Of all the days to invite me out, thought Jemma. She checked the clock. Five to five. 'We may as well close up,' she said. 'It won't take long.' She cashed up quickly, noting that there wasn't much actual money in the till. The sales had all been paid for with credit cards.

'I'll head off, if you don't mind,' said Maddy, on the first stroke of five.

'Yes, see you tomorrow,' said Jemma, unable to put any feeling into her voice. Once Maddy had gone she looked at Carl. 'I don't want to go for a drink,' she said. 'I'm not in the mood. I'm sorry to make you wait, but I didn't want to say it in front of Maddy.'

'What's up?' said Carl. 'You seem really down.'

'I can't run this place,' said Jemma. 'I'm not making the right decisions. It isn't working. I put the wrong books in the window. Maddy knows what to do, and I don't, but I'm stuck with it. And I'm worried about—' She stopped herself just in time. Raphael wouldn't want her to discuss his problems. 'I'm worried,' she finished.

'I'm worried too,' said Carl. 'About you. You haven't given me the time of day for the last week or so.'

'That isn't my fault,' Jemma retorted. 'You've been busy.' *And so have I*, she thought. *Though I might as well not have bothered.*

'There you go again,' said Carl. 'Why are you being so negative? And why haven't you answered my texts?'

'What texts?' said Jemma. 'I wasn't aware that you'd sent any.'

'Course I have,' said Carl. 'Look.' He pulled his phone out of his jeans pocket and brought up a stream of messages. 'See?'

Jemma looked.

Monday, 7.55 am: Room for one more for breakfast?

Monday, 5.15 pm: Fancy a coffee? I know a place :-)

Tuesday, 8.30 am: I miss scrambled eggs :-(

Wednesday, 4.30 pm: You could come and watch us rehearse. If you like.

Jemma reached for her own phone, and showed him. 'I haven't had a text from you all week,' she said. 'Not since Saturday. I thought you were busy.'

'I was,' said Carl, 'but not that busy.' He frowned. 'That's weird. What network are you on?'

Jemma checked his phone. 'Same as you,' she said. 'I

don't get it. I'm sure I searched for stuff on the internet, and that worked fine.'

Carl's mouth curled in a wry smile. 'At least now I know you weren't ignoring me.' A sidelong glance. 'Unless you would have anyway.'

'Of course I wouldn't,' cried Jemma. She felt the unfairness of it welling up inside her. 'It's not my fault. At least that's one thing that isn't my fault—'

Then she was in Carl's arms, and weeping as if she would never stop.

'Come on,' whispered Carl, after a minute or two. 'Let's lock the shop and go upstairs, and you can tell me all about it.' And Jemma was too exhausted to do anything but agree.

***

'It wasn't the drink I had in mind,' said Carl, as Jemma handed him a mug of tea with three sugars. 'But it's lovely,' he added hastily, as her lower lip wobbled. 'It's just nice to see you. I mean, I've seen you in the bookshop but you've been all stridey-about and managerial.'

'Not that it helps,' said Jemma. She sat down on the chesterfield sofa and sipped her tea reflectively. 'I've been swanning around as if I know what I'm doing, and obviously I don't.'

'But you do,' said Carl. 'Look at what you've done at Burns Books. Raphael is full of praise for you.'

Jemma snorted. 'I got lucky,' she said.

'Oh come on,' said Carl. 'No one is that lucky for that long. Please, Jemma. Please tell me what's up.'

He paused, then reached out a hand to her. 'I know you

don't want to talk about it, but it might help.' He smiled. 'How many acting jobs do you think I haven't got? How many times do you think I've been turned away because I'm too tall, or too young, or my hair is wrong, or I'm not what they're looking for? Believe me, I know all about rejection.'

After her initial resistance, Jemma told him. It was over so quickly that she wondered whether she'd left anything out.

'That's . . . kind of interesting,' said Carl.

'I don't need a critique of my business strategy,' Jemma snapped. 'I've had quite enough of that from my assistant, thanks.'

Carl grinned. 'I'm hardly qualified to comment on that,' he said, 'but I can comment on the words you used. Everything is about what you *don't* want. Almost every verb you use suggests conflict. You're fighting, you're struggling, you're losing. You keep telling me that you're wrong, you're mistaken, you don't know, you don't understand.'

Jemma hung her head. 'I don't understand,' she muttered.

'But you do,' said Carl. 'You understand how you want the shop to work. You know how you want the shop to be. And instead of going for it you're changing little things here and there: just enough to wind Maddy up, but not enough to achieve what you want. Stop thinking about the customers you don't want, and the books you'd rather not sell. Think about the people you do want to sell to, and the books they'll like.'

'I'm wading through treacle the whole time,' said Jemma. 'I thought I was getting somewhere with Maddy and she was finally coming round to my point of view. Then she pulls a stunt like this morning's, changing my display the minute I go out.'

'So tell her that's unacceptable,' said Carl. 'She can't do that. It's your shop.'

'But it doesn't feel as if it is,' said Jemma, shifting uncomfortably on the firm leather. 'I try to tell myself it is, but it still feels like Brian's. I'm just making a mess of it until he comes back.'

'So do something about it,' said Carl. 'Do something to make it yours.' He gazed around the beautiful, elegant room. 'To be honest, Jemma, lovely as this flat is, it doesn't feel like your home. It feels as if you're flat-sitting.'

Jemma sighed out a breath. Then she picked up a cushion with a sunburst on, which she had brought from her own flat, and hugged it. 'I thought I'd get used to it,' she said quietly. 'I thought it was just a bit more sophisticated than I was used to, and I'd grow into it. But it isn't me, not at all.'

Carl reached for the pink fleecy throw and draped it over the sofa. 'It's a start.'

Jemma managed a shaky smile. 'It is,' she said. Then she glanced at the carriage clock that she'd never liked. 'Aren't you rehearsing tonight?'

Carl looked at her. 'I'm supposed to be,' he said. 'They've got scripts, they can manage without me. If you want me to stay—'

'To be honest,' said Jemma, 'what I'd really like is to

get out of this flat, and the shop. Could I come and watch?'

Carl beamed. 'Sure you can,' he said. 'Now we're getting somewhere with it, I'd love to see what you think.' A sudden, shy smile. 'I thought you weren't interested.'

'Of course I'm interested,' said Jemma, 'it's your thing. Come on, let's get out of here.' She got up from the sofa and held out her hand. 'Have we got time for food first?'

Carl grinned. 'You're definitely feeling better.'

It's amazing what a difference someone else's view makes, thought Jemma, as they strolled down Charing Cross Road hand-in-hand. Now she was bursting with things to get on with, both in the shop and in her flat. But all that could wait until tomorrow. First, she had something far more pressing to do.

Chapter 10

Jemma woke with a pleasing sense of anticipation. *Today's the day.* She reached out and smoothed the duvet cover. It wasn't one of the superfine Egyptian cotton duvet covers which Brian favoured, but a slightly faded Indian sari-print one she had bought in the sales years ago, when she was getting things for her first flat. *It may not be posh*, she thought, stroking the soft, slightly pilled fabric, *but it's mine.*

Watching Rumpus the night before had been a strange, out-of-body experience. She had known beforehand that Carl's play was set in a bookshop, and she had also known that they were rehearsing downstairs at Burns Books. But seeing it, seeing characters move around the shop being customers or staff, and handling the books as if they worked there, was bizarre. *Almost as if I'm a ghost haunting the place. I really should develop some outside interests.*

She had worried that the setting would remind her of the day's events; but Carl's small cast of characters was so well-drawn, so real, and so different from herself, Maddy and Raphael that she had no difficulty in sinking into the drama, to the extent that she was cross when one of the actors fluffed their lines, or when Carl, who was directing, stopped the action to give notes.

'Did you enjoy it?' Carl asked her afterwards, when the rest of Rumpus had dispersed and he was making his usual checks before locking up. He asked the question when he was busy locking the toilet door.

'Don't be silly,' she said, from the front-row armchair where she had acted as their audience. 'Of course I did. I'm not just saying that because I'm – you know.' The word *girlfriend* stuck in her throat. *Partner*, too. 'Because we go out,' she finished.

He turned to her then, and smiled. 'We do,' he said. 'I'm glad you liked it. I was – a bit worried.'

'Why wouldn't I have liked it?' said Jemma. 'It was funny, it was moving—'

Carl raised his hands, palms upwards, then let them fall. 'The others say the same, but I still worry. Call it imposter syndrome. It's the first time I've written a whole actual play. We improvised sketches at uni, but this is different. This feels big: serious. The idea of putting on an actual thing that I wrote—'

Jemma grinned. 'The play what I wrote,' she said.

Carl grinned back at her. 'This play is like my shop window. I'm putting my work out there and worrying that people will decide it's not their thing, and I'm no good—'

Jemma walked over, touched his arm, and kissed him. 'Let's go for that drink,' she said.

***

They had made it one drink then parted company, since Jemma had plans for what was left of the evening. As soon as she got home she changed the bed. *I can't bear to sleep in his sheets any more.* Then she went to the big cupboard where she had stored everything she had brought from her previous flat which didn't fit with the new one. Big bright towels that looked incongruous in the tasteful bathroom. Framed posters, some from her student days, which had seemed unsophisticated compared to Brian's art prints and watercolours. The scented candles in glass holders she had bought from IKEA, and the bundle of postcards which she had stuck to her fridge with souvenir magnets. She brought it all out, and stared at it.

Not everything, she thought, picking up a particularly horrible pottery rabbit which her mother had brought back from somewhere or other. *But this, and this—*

She moved around the flat, taking down pictures and replacing them with her own. A couple, which she liked, she moved to a different room. Brian's placemats, featuring scenes from Renaissance Italy, were replaced with her multicoloured woven straw ones. The abstract ceramic figures on the mantelpiece, which unnerved her every time she looked at them, were boxed and put away. And the deep-pile pale-beige rug in the sitting room, which she never walked on for fear of making it dirty, was rolled up, and a more colourful and forgiving rag rug laid in its place.

Jemma picked up the carriage clock; the hands said it was a quarter to midnight. *I'd better stop there*, she thought, carrying the clock to the cupboard and swaddling it in a pillowcase to muffle it until it wound down. She closed the door and locked it, and suddenly she could have floated away, she felt so light. As if she could do anything she wanted.

***

Jemma moved easily around the flat, getting breakfast. She smothered her guilt that she was scrambling her eggs in Brian's heavy copper saucepan instead of one of her own cheap ones. *That's my choice*, she thought. *Maybe when I'm earning more money I'll replace this with one of my own.* That made her smile.

She even managed a smile for Maddy when she came into the shop. 'Good morning, Maddy,' she said.

'Good morning,' said Maddy warily, her eyes searching Jemma's face for signs of trouble.

'Let's get on with things, shall we?' said Jemma.

'Yes,' said Maddy, and bit her lip. 'We are a little low on stock—'

'Oh, because you've been selling so many books,' said Jemma. Maddy gave her a quick glance, as if trying to winkle out a hidden, sarcastic meaning. 'Well, I'm planning to go and see Raphael today, and that's on my list.'

'Oh,' said Maddy. She picked up a couple of auction catalogues and handed them to Jemma. 'Brian used to go to these regularly, and some other dealers. I can give you their addresses if you want.'

'Yes please, that would be helpful,' said Jemma. Maddy drew out a small black book from the drawer under the counter, and began leafing through it. 'I'll go and put the kettle on,' Jemma continued. 'I might wait until Raphael's got a good amount of caffeine inside him before I head over.'

An odd sort of bark shot out of Maddy and made Jemma jump. Then she realised it was a laugh. Maddy looked as surprised as she felt. 'What will you ask him?' she said.

'I'd like his advice about buying books,' Jemma replied. 'I'm a bit worried that otherwise I'll get fleeced.'

'Oh yes, very wise,' said Maddy. 'Always good to consult an expert. Although the names I've given you should help a lot.'

'I'm sure they will,' said Jemma. 'And there are a couple of other things I want to ask him. Anyway, tea.' She went into the kitchen and filled the kettle. She felt guilty that she had no intention of using the information that Maddy had vouchsafed to her. But not very.

***

She found Raphael upstairs doing the crossword, while Folio snoozed in a patch of bright autumn sunlight. 'How are things?' she asked.

Raphael considered. 'The bookshop's doing well,' he said.

'I know it is,' said Jemma automatically. Then she noted his emphasis on the word *bookshop*. 'How about you?'

Raphael sighed. 'Still fielding criticism of my, what was

it, namby-pamby people-pleasing gone-to-the-dogs recruitment process.'

'Oh dear,' said Jemma.

'Yes dear,' said Raphael. He waved a hand. 'Anyway, what brings you here?'

'I want to repaint the exterior of the shop,' said Jemma. 'And give it a new name, and buy plenty of books for it.'

'I see,' said Raphael. 'So the new stock's selling well, then?'

'I haven't put it out yet,' Jemma confessed, and explained the reason why. 'Carl made me see that I should make a proper change, not just tinker round the edges.'

'I see,' said Raphael. 'Carl, eh?'

'He's smart,' said Jemma, indignantly.

'I never said he wasn't,' said Raphael. 'So are you telling me, or asking me?'

'I'm asking you,' said Jemma. 'I wouldn't presume to rename and repaint your shop without your permission.'

'And if I said no,' said Raphael, 'what would you do?'

Jemma studied him, but his words seemed hypothetical. She could feel a smile trying to get out. 'I'd attempt to talk you round.'

'Of course you would,' said Raphael. 'And for the record, you're doing the right thing. What I would suggest is that you don't pick a colour or a name that you're likely to get tired of.' He paused. 'Do you have something in mind?'

'Not yet,' admitted Jemma. 'I was just thinking not black and not BJF Antiquarian Books.' She slapped her forehead. 'Which is exactly what Carl told me I was doing.

Being negative.' Then she looked at Raphael. 'Actually, that might help you,' she said.

'Might it?' said Raphael.

'Yes,' said Jemma. 'You're firefighting at the moment, aren't you? Dealing with people's negative feedback and what they don't want, and *you* don't want that either. Maybe if you focused on telling them what you hope to get out of making the changes, they'd understand.'

'Oh,' said Raphael. 'I did say I was doing this so that I didn't hire another Brian.' He mused. 'Good heavens.'

'We both need to reframe our narratives,' said Jemma.

Raphael winced. 'What I need is a nice cappuccino.'

'You know what,' said Jemma, 'you could be right.'

***

Over cappuccinos and a biscotti each at Rolando's, Raphael outlined the dos and don'ts of buying stock, and gave her three names. One was a house-clearance man with a warehouse in Putney; one was a secondhand book dealer in Colindale; and the third, according to Raphael, had no profession. 'I would call her a snapper-up of unconsidered trifles,' he said. 'She is more expensive, but if you're seeking a particular volume she's sure to have it. Very important when you're making a set.' He sat back. 'What sort of stock are you looking for, anyway?'

'Books I want to read,' said Jemma. 'Not necessarily books that I have read, but books I'd like to read someday. And books that look nice on the shelves. It's hard to explain, but I'll know it when I see it.'

'You'll know it when you feel it,' said Raphael. He drained his cappuccino and Giulia appeared at his elbow.

'Un altro?' she asked.

'Sì, grazie,' said Raphael, and smiled at her. She laid a hand on his shoulder briefly, then picked up his cup and was gone.

Jemma frowned. 'Are you two…?'

'She is a lovely person,' said Raphael, 'and smart as a whip. Under different circumstances…' He muttered something and Jemma caught the last few words: 'couldn't go through it again.'

'But would you make each other happy?' she asked, very quietly and very gently.

Raphael shrugged. 'Probably. For a little while.' And then he looked sad, until Giulia reappeared with another cappuccino with two little Gianduja chocolates tucked into the saucer. 'One for you,' she said to Jemma, pointing at the chocolates, then at her. 'Don't let him eat both.' And with a chuckle, she was gone.

'I'm saying nothing,' said Jemma, helping herself to a chocolate. 'You know what I think.' She unwrapped it and took a bite.

'Everything is so simple when you're young,' said Raphael, wistfully. 'Even now I can remember it.' He took a sip of his cappuccino. 'But I think you're right about my problem.' He smiled. 'So, thank you.'

Jemma took a convoluted route back to her shop, which passed the hardware store. There she grabbed all the paint catalogues she could lay hands on, and popped them in her bag. *I'll look at them over lunch and pick out some colours. And I can think about a name while Maddy serves the customers.* A secret naughty thrill ran through her, as if she were planning to get something past a teacher, or possibly her mother. *I should just do it,* she thought. *Openly, in front of Maddy, so that she knows what's going to happen.*

Then she considered, and grinned. *Actually,* she admitted to herself, *I like the idea that I'm sneaking this in under Maddy's nose. Maybe it's because it feels as if I'm outwitting Brian.* Outwitting Brian, she had to admit, was a delightful thought. Almost as delightful as the thought that soon, very soon, she would have a bookshop arranged exactly the way she wanted it.

Chapter 11

'Are you sure you don't want me to come?' said Raphael.

'I'll be fine,' said Jemma. 'Driving is like riding a bike; you never forget how. I promise I'll look after Gertrude.' She jingled the keys, hoping she appeared less apprehensive than she felt. She was a good driver – no accidents, no speeding tickets – though an infrequent one. And she had never driven a vehicle as big as Gertrude. However, she was unlikely to have to parallel park or do a three-point turn in a narrow road. 'Slow and steady wins the race,' she added.

'I was thinking more of the book-buying aspect of the expedition,' said Raphael. 'As you know, I do like a trip out.' He sighed. 'I suppose you must start sometime. One's first solo book-buying trip is a rite of passage.'

'Don't make me more nervous than I already am,' said Jemma. 'Now, I've got the addresses, my phone is fully charged, and you're sure they'll send the bill to the shop?'

'As you said approximately two minutes ago, Jemma, it'll be fine,' said Raphael. 'Off you go, and enjoy yourself.'

'And if you bring back any copies of *Fifty Shades of Grey*, we won't let you in,' said Luke, grinning.

Jemma rolled her eyes. 'You're cheerful,' she said. 'And rather smart.' The midnight-blue shirt had made a reappearance, teamed with snazzy black trousers with a thin black satin stripe down the side. 'Another date tonight?'

Luke looked away, then gave her a little sidelong glance. 'Might be.'

'Are you leaving today or tomorrow?' asked Raphael. Just then, the shop bell rang. 'Good, a customer. Off you go, and stop disrupting my shop. I expect to hear all about it when you get back.'

'You will,' said Jemma. 'And thank you.' She smiled at the customer and hurried out. Gertrude was waiting, her bright orange paint shining in the mellow autumn sunlight as if she were a giant pumpkin.

Jemma had popped downstairs earlier and asked Carl to stay there when she left the shop. 'I know you want to see me off,' she said. 'But you'll say something encouraging or motivational, and I don't want to cry in front of the others.'

'Who, me?' said Carl, with a cheesy grin. 'Motivational? All right then, I guess I'll just have to do it now.' He folded her in a big hug, and whispered, 'Go do your thing, and be awesome.'

'Aargh!' cried Jemma, but it was too late; she could already feel tears welling up, and his hug squeezed them out of her even faster. 'I'm happy, really I am,' she hiccupped.

And here she was, bowling along in Gertrude, with the maps app on her phone set to Putney. *The roads seem quiet.* She had expected to crawl out of the city, but somehow all the traffic lights changed to green as she approached them, and the bits of road coloured red on her map faded to orange, then their usual colour as she drove along them. *Hmmm*, she thought, and rubbed Gertrude's steering wheel.

Her mood was further improved by the knowledge that the painters would arrive that afternoon. Having obtained three quotes, Jemma had gone with the cheapest, from the firm that Raphael used. 'They've been in business for two hundred years,' he had said. 'They know what they're doing.'

On one hand, Jemma hoped that she would be out when they arrived, so that she wouldn't face the initial wrath of Maddy. Then again, she didn't want to miss seeing the look on Maddy's face when they arrived and started unpacking their equipment. After much thought she had gone for a deep, rich burgundy which was still bookshop-ish and classy, but much warmer and brighter than the current dull black. As for a name – unable to settle on anything, she had booked a signwriter for two days' time, on the grounds that that would make her come to a decision.

Almost before she knew it, she was in Putney. Gertrude rolled down quiet leafy streets until eventually they came to a long, low warehouse, nothing special to look at. 'You have arrived at your destination,' the phone declared.

A tall, skinny, balding man in faded jeans and a voluminous shirt sauntered outside. 'Hello, Gertrude,' he said, rubbing her wing mirror. 'Jemma James, I presume,' he said, extending a hand to her. 'I'm Dave Huddart. I gather you're after books.'

'I am,' said Jemma. She dismounted from Gertrude and pulled a long list out of her bag.

Dave took the list and scanned it rapidly. 'Yep,' he said. 'Got boxes?'

'Oh yes,' said Jemma. 'And the trolley.'

'All prepared, then.' He twinkled at her. 'First time?'

'Is it that obvious?' said Jemma, fighting the urge to take a step back.

'Nah,' said Dave. 'You've just got that look about you. If you get your things and come this way, I'll take you to the book department.'

He led Jemma through an Aladdin's cave. To the left bristled a forest of chairs. To her right, a small army of mannequin heads wearing elaborate hats stared with sightless eyes. Then lamps and lights of all descriptions, some lit but most not, gleamed in their dark home.

'I'm afraid things aren't in order,' said Dave. 'I've split the fiction and non-fiction, but that's about it.'

Don't go mad, Jemma cautioned herself, as she gazed at the shelves. *This is your first shop. Only choose things you're sure will sell.*

'I'll come back in ten minutes and see how you're getting on,' said Dave.

Jemma undropped her jaw long enough to say thank

you, then continued to gawp at the shelves.

You've seen a lot of books before, she told herself. *There probably aren't as many here as there are in the stockroom at Burns Books. Or on the lower floor, come to that.* But somehow these books, crammed into shelves, on top of shelves, in piles at the foot of shelves, had an impact all their own. 'Folio would love this,' she said aloud. Timidly, she reached out for a hardback copy of Hans Christian Andersen's fairy tales. When she held the book in her hand, she knew she would buy it. 'This is so tempting,' she whispered, putting the book on a small table which stood nearby. 'And so dangerous.'

Jemma decided to limit herself to five boxes. She chose carefully, visualising the book on her shelves, or turned so that its cover faced the customer, and considering how it would complement her other selections. Even so, she had amassed a good four boxes' worth when Dave reappeared. 'Found some stuff, then,' he said.

'Could I have two more minutes?' asked Jemma.

He laughed. 'I think that's safe. Any more than that, and I suspect you'd buy the whole shop.' He stood by as she chose twenty more books, her hands shooting out confidently, stroking the books as she laid them down. 'Want me to price that lot up?'

Jemma blinked. 'I'm not sure.' She blinked. Now that she had been brought back to reality, she did seem to have chosen an awful lot of books. Very nice books. 'Um, can I put some back if I'm over budget?'

Dave frowned, then laughed. 'Course you can. Give me a minute.' He crooked his forefinger and waggled it as he scrutinised the spines of the books, muttering to himself all the while. Jemma heard numbers, and words like *original slipcase* and *colour plates*, and her heart sank. What if she had to put half of them back? She felt as if it would break her heart.

Then Dave said a number, and she stared at him. 'Excuse me?'

He said it again.

'Are you sure? For all these books?'

'Yep,' said Dave. 'I've got books coming out of my ears and you'll be a good customer. And you're a referral from Raphael, which counts for something.' He grinned at her. 'I take it you're happy with that?'

'Are you kidding me?' said Jemma, grinning from ear to ear. She held out her hand. 'Let's shake on it, before you change your mind.'

Dave helped her pack the boxes, and she wheeled her new acquisitions over to Gertrude with a spring in her step. *I can see why Raphael enjoys this part of his job. It's like being a kid in a sweet shop, only less fattening.*

She selected another three boxes' worth at the secondhand bookshop in Colindale. Here the prices were keener, though the owner was as nice and as welcoming as Dave, in his own way. At first sight he had looked rather forbidding: like the first Doctor Who, in fact. But he made her tea in a china cup, and his melodious, slightly cracked voice rose and fell like a gentle sea as he told tales of authors he had met while Jemma chose her books. She felt as if she were bobbing in a small boat, surrounded by soft cushions.

She was in two minds whether or not to bother with the third name on Raphael's list. 'I have plenty of books already,' she argued as she drove towards the city. 'Raphael did say she was expensive.'

But it wouldn't hurt to look, said an eager voice in her head. *It's on the way back. You won't even be going out of your way.*

If Jemma could have stared at herself, she would. She was so used to her inner voice being critical and negative that this was something entirely new. As such, she ought to encourage it. So she pulled over at the next opportunity, and put the final address into her phone.

To her surprise, she drew up at an ordinary semi-detached house. She gazed doubtfully at the phone, which looked reasonably sure of itself. And the number on the white PVC front door was correct. Slightly deflated, Jemma got out of Gertrude and walked up the neat garden path.

The door was answered by a middle-aged woman slightly smaller than Jemma. She was plump, and dressed in a pale-blue top, a beige skirt, and fluffy pink slippers. 'Good afternoon,' she said, in an unexpectedly deep voice. 'I take it you're here about books.'

Jemma made a couple of fishlike motions with her mouth before managing to form words. 'Yes, that's right.'

'Anything in particular?'

'I'm relaunching my bookshop and adding fiction,' said Jemma. Inwardly, she frowned. That wasn't what she had meant to say.

'Oh, so you want a book which says exactly what your

new bookshop will be about.' The woman's gaze wandered for a moment, then refocused on Jemma. 'If you wait in the hall, I believe I have what you're looking for.' She paused. 'Who am I speaking to, by the way?'

'Jemma James,' Jemma stammered.

The woman inclined her head and opened the door wider. 'I am Elinor Dashwood. Yes, I know.' She stepped back, showing Jemma a completely unexceptional hall with laminate flooring and a waiting-room type chair. 'If you'll take a seat.'

It took Jemma perhaps thirty seconds to take in her surroundings. A dark-wood telephone table, a barometer on the wall, Constable prints, and pale striped wallpaper. In its own way, it was by far the strangest of the three establishments she had visited that day.

'Here we are,' said Elinor Dashwood, emerging from what looked like a dining room. 'Rather nice, if I do say so myself.' She put the book into Jemma's hands. 'Preowned, of course, but in mint condition.'

Jemma gazed at it. The book was a hardback, bound in beautiful blue silk that made you want to stroke it. Set into the cover, in swirling silver script, was the book's title: *Jane Eyre.* The first book she had ever sold. She opened it and found marbled endpapers, a blue silk ribbon bookmark, and delicate engravings.

'It's absolutely beautiful,' she said. 'How much is it?'

'It is beautiful,' said Elinor Dashwood. 'But it isn't a first edition, it isn't by a famous binder, and it was published by a little-known company. It is also a duplicate; I have two of these. So I could let you have it for fifteen pounds.'

Jemma fumbled for her purse. 'Done.' She could already see it in the shop window. *Her* shop window. 'I'll be back,' she said, as Elinor opened the drawer of the telephone table and brought out a sheet of tissue paper.

'I know you will,' said Elinor.

Jemma drove the few miles to Charing Cross Road almost in a trance. *What a day it's been, and it isn't even over yet.* It was one o'clock, she had visited three booksellers and bought books from all of them, and she was still, just about, within her budget. And she would have time for lunch before the painters arrived.

Or so she thought. For when she pulled up outside BJF Antiquarian Books, the painters' van was already there. More worryingly, the painters were getting into it. She switched Gertrude's engine off, and as if on cue, the engine of the van coughed into life.

'Wait! No!' she shouted. Then, realising that was no use, she jumped out of Gertrude, ran to the driver's side of the van, heedless of traffic, and knocked on the window. She could see the frown on the driver's face even before he wound it down. *What's been going on?*

Chapter 12

'Got our marching orders, didn't we,' said the driver, putting the van into gear.

'No you didn't,' said Jemma, with desperation. 'I'm the manager.'

'The woman we spoke to in there made it clear that we weren't expected or welcome,' snapped the driver. 'To be honest with you, after what she said I wouldn't stay.'

'Please stay,' said Jemma. 'I don't know what Maddy said to you, but I shall make sure she apologises.'

The driver muttered something which sounded like 'She'd ruddy better,' put the van into neutral, and switched off the engine.

'Thank you,' said Jemma. 'I'm sorry I wasn't here to welcome you, but I thought you were coming at two o'clock.'

'Job before finished early,' put in the man next to the

driver. 'Thought we'd get a jump on this one.' He peered out of the window at the shop, and turned back with a critical expression on his face. 'We'll need to.' He got out of the van and looked up at the building, wrinkling his nose.

The driver sighed and leaned out of his window. 'You could at least unload the stuff,' he said.

'Thank you so much,' said Jemma. 'Would you like some tea?'

She had to jump back as the door opened. The driver got out and slammed it. 'Haven't done anything yet,' he said, shielding his eyes as he scrutinised the building. 'Burgundy, was it?'

'That's it,' said Jemma, feeling rather in the way. 'I'll, um, go and talk to Maddy.'

She had expected Maddy to be deep in conversation with a favourite customer, but when she entered, the shop was empty. Maddy was sitting at the counter, flicking through an auction catalogue and eating something worthy-looking in a box. She glanced up when Jemma closed the door. 'Oh, hello.'

'Would you mind telling me,' said Jemma, putting her hands on her hips, 'why you sent the painters away, and what exactly you said to them? It's lucky I got here when I did, otherwise they would have taken off.'

Maddy waved her fork while she chewed. 'The shop's fine as it is.'

Her offhand tone stung Jemma. 'Well, I say that it isn't. I'm in charge and I have Raphael's backing, so what I say goes, whatever your opinion is.' She stalked up to the counter. 'What did you say to them?'

Maddy shrugged. 'I told the head one that the shop didn't need painting, and that as far as I was concerned they were a bunch of crooks looking to swindle an inexperienced shop manager.'

'You what?' cried Jemma. 'How dare you!'

Maddy put down her fork, a cold glint in her eyes. 'Do you think that under your management the shop is earning enough for an expensive makeover? Do you really?'

'Maybe if I had an assistant who supported me, instead of sticking to the ways of her former and now departed boss, we might get somewhere.' Jemma could feel herself swelling with rage. 'Firstly, you will go and apologise to the painters for calling them crooks, and tell them that you were wrong. Then you will help me unload the new books I have bought for the shop. And finally, you will accept the changes I make in the shop, or else hand in your notice. I'm not having any more of this.' She gazed around her. 'I've a good mind to rip out this shelving and put in something a bit less dark and depressing.'

Maddy gasped and hurried outside. Jemma followed, and stood in the doorway while Maddy choked an apology out, 'I'm-sorry-for-calling-you-crooks-I-was-wrong.' That done, she dashed inside so quickly that Jemma had to step out of the way, and bolted for the staff toilet.

Five minutes later she still hadn't emerged. *Was I too harsh?* thought Jemma, as she stood in the middle of the shop and waited.

She insulted people who came to do a job for you, and managed to be dismissive of you in the process. She's lucky you didn't give her a warning.

Don't tempt me, thought Jemma. But she still watched the door.

Maddy reappeared ten more minutes later. Her eyes were red-rimmed, and she wore a slight, perplexed frown. 'I don't feel well,' she said.

'Mmm,' said Jemma. 'You'll excuse me if I'm not particularly sympathetic towards you at the moment, Maddy.' Then she relented, as Maddy did look genuinely confused. 'What is it?' she said.

'I'm not myself.' Maddy put a hand to her head.

'Why don't you take your lunch break and go out for some fresh air,' said Jemma. 'Maybe that will help.'

'Thank you,' said Maddy, quietly. She fetched her bag and hurried across the shop floor, stumbling in her haste to leave.

The door closed behind her, and Jemma pondered. Was it a not-very-cunning ploy to get out of unloading the books? Somehow, she didn't think so. To be honest, she would have been perfectly happy to send Maddy out of the shop for an hour after a much less convincing performance, simply to recover her own composure. Perhaps Maddy's anger had brought on a headache; it was perfectly possible to feel sick with nerves, wasn't it? But Maddy's expression – bewildered, helpless, lost – had struck at Jemma in a completely unexpected way. *I'll try to be kinder when she comes back*, she thought. *I don't want to fall out with her if I can help it. I don't want to be that kind of manager.* Instead, she spent the next half an hour unloading boxes of books from the van and stacking them beside the counter. She had no idea where they would go yet, but she intended to enjoy every minute of sorting, organising, and shelving her new acquisitions.

***

Jemma felt a stab of misgiving even as she handed Gertrude's keys to Raphael. Had she done the right thing? Could she trust Maddy?

'Did it go well?' asked Raphael. 'You seem rather burdened with care, if I may say so.'

'What? Oh, sorry. Yes, it went really well. I bought eight boxes of books and they were actually much less expensive than I thought they would be. I got a beautiful copy of *Jane Eyre* from Elinor Dashwood.'

Raphael smiled knowingly. 'So you haven't been too scarred by the experience?'

'No, not at all. Um, would you mind if I went back there now? It's just that I've left Maddy in charge of the shop, and I'd like to get things organised for tomorrow if I can. I'll tell you more about it once I've got the shop straightened up.'

'Make sure you do,' said Raphael. 'Did you meet Dave's parrot?'

'Dave's parrot? No, I definitely didn't see a parrot.'

'Just checking. Off you go then.'

As Jemma hurried out of Burns Books she wondered at the expression in his eyes. Pride? Wistfulness? She couldn't tell. Anyway, she needed to check on Maddy. She had only been away for ten minutes at the most, but ten minutes with Maddy in charge of the shop was a very long time indeed.

98

When Maddy had returned from her break her face seemed less drawn, she had colour in her cheeks, and she looked thoroughly ashamed of herself. 'I'm sorry,' she said, advancing to the counter and meeting Jemma's eyes. 'I don't know what came over me to speak as I did. Unless it's all the change. I didn't think it would affect me so much, but obviously it has.'

'Change can be difficult to get used to,' said Jemma, with the wisdom acquired from hours of diligent study and course attendance. 'I should have warned you that they were coming. It wasn't fair of me to spring it on you like that. I'll do better in future.'

Maddy managed a wan smile. 'Are we friends again?'

Jemma's first thought was that their relationship was one of manager and employee, not friends, but Maddy looked so pathetic with her little hopeful smile that she dismissed the thought as unworthy. 'Sure,' she said. 'Shall we make a drink, and think about where these books will go?'

She had already redone the window display, which to be honest was a matter of taking the expensive spotlighted book out of the window and replacing it with a mix of attractive and reasonably priced offerings, with the beautiful hardback *Jane Eyre* at the centre. To appease Maddy, she had included some non-fiction in the mix.

'I'll go and put the kettle on,' said Maddy. On her way into the back, she hesitated. 'I like the window. And the painters are getting on well with the prep work.'

'Good, I thought they would,' said Jemma. 'They did come recommended.'

While Maddy was making drinks, Jemma considered the shelves. To emphasise the shop's change of direction, the new books ought to be at the front. She unlocked the doors of the first bookcase and began clearing the shelves. She should probably alphabetise the new books, but that could wait; she was too eager to make the change. By the time Maddy returned bearing drinks, Jemma had filled two shelves of the bookcase and was beginning the third. 'I've started,' she said. 'I haven't put them in order. It's just for now.'

Maddy's left hand trembled a fraction, but she didn't look angry. If anything, she looked enquiring, as if she were trying to make sense of it. She opened her mouth, and closed it again. Eventually, she spoke. 'I don't suppose . . . I don't suppose you found any Ann Radcliffe?'

'I didn't,' said Jemma. 'I did keep an eye out.' That was a little white lie, but she was fairly confident that she had seen no Radcliffe novels that morning, which was almost the same thing.

Maddy put the mugs on the counter. 'Shall I clear the next bookcase?'

Jemma tried not to stare at her. 'Yes please, that would be helpful,' she said. 'I guess I'm doing this the wrong way round, but I can't wait to see the new books in the shop.' She crossed to the counter and took a sip of her tea, regarding the shelves. Already it was more colourful. And she wouldn't lock the doors when she'd finished. Maybe she would even get the glass removed.

Half an hour later two bookcases were full of new books, and the previous inhabitants were packed and heading for the stockroom. 'I'll update the database, I promise,' said Jemma. 'Um, would you mind if I nipped upstairs and got myself some toast? I haven't eaten since breakfast.'

'Oh no, that's fine,' said Maddy. 'If you like, I can get on with putting the new books into the database.'

Jemma took the stairs two at a time, wondering at Maddy's sudden turnaround. She had been prepared for hostility and possibly hard words, but instead Maddy had taken it more or less in her stride. She hadn't looked mutinous, which pleased Jemma. She had wanted to help, and shown interest in Jemma's plans.

'I give up,' said Jemma, and put two slices of bread into the toaster. She only hoped that when she went downstairs she wouldn't find that Maddy had flipped and begun feeding her new prized possessions into the shredder.

When she did re-enter the shop she found Maddy listening to a customer, an elderly gentleman with a monocle whom Jemma was convinced she had never seen in the shop before. 'So this is your new manager,' he said to Maddy, scrutinising Jemma through the monocle, which made his eye look alarmingly large. 'Making changes, I see. I don't believe in change for change's sake, but it's interesting. How much is that *Jane Eyre* in the window?'

Jemma was tempted to tell him that the book wasn't for sale, but fought her urge to keep it. 'I haven't priced it yet. How much would you be prepared to pay for a book like that?'

'If you fetch it out of the window, I'll tell you.' He rocked on his heels while he waited.

Jemma laid the book on the counter. She couldn't work out whether she wanted him to snap it up or say that it wasn't quite what he was looking for. If he rejected it—

He adjusted his monocle so that his eye grew even bigger, and opened the cover. Then he leafed through a few pages, opened the book gently to the middle, and examined the binding and the ribbon. 'I'd expect to see this in a bookshop for about fifty pounds,' he said. 'As I've done you the favour of assessing it for you, perhaps you would accept forty.'

Jemma blinked.

Maddy gazed at the gentleman. 'Shall we split the difference, and say forty-five?'

He frowned, and for a moment Jemma feared the monocle would crack. Then he chuckled, said, 'I suppose we have to make a living,' and drew an ancient leather wallet from his trouser pocket.

Once he had left, Maddy said, 'Which book should we put into the display?'

'Why don't you choose,' said Jemma. And as Maddy advanced to the new books, slowly Jemma shook her head. One day she would understand people; but today was not that day.

Chapter 13

'May I go for lunch?' asked Maddy.

Jemma glanced at the clock. Was it really only a quarter past twelve? She felt as if she had been working for at least six hours. 'Sure.'

'Thanks,' said Maddy. She collected her bag and her coat, a short, stone-coloured mac, and made for the door.

Before she could reach it, it opened and Luke stepped in. 'Hello, Maddy,' he said, pausing as they came face to face.

'Hello, Luke,' said Maddy, and looked quickly away.

Luke stepped aside and held the door open for her. 'Thank you,' murmured Maddy, and scurried off, head down. Was Jemma mistaken, or were her normally pale cheeks rather pink?

'Hi, Jemma,' said Luke. 'How's it going?'

Jemma had maintained the same erect, straight-backed

posture all morning. She found she could hold it no longer, and slumped over the counter. 'I'm knackered,' she said.

'Business is booming, then?' Luke advanced to the counter and leaned on it, facing her.

'I'm doing my best,' said Jemma.

A week ago, Jemma had gone on her book-buying expedition and returned to find Maddy banishing the painters. Since then, the shop had been repainted and she had chosen a name.

It had taken many sheets of A4 paper, filled with evocative words and synonyms which eventually were all scored through. Some were too ambitious, some too ambiguous, some too specific. Sitting at the dining table in her flat upstairs, Jemma heard the grandfather clock strike midnight as she crumpled another sheet of paper and threw it in the bin. Finally, at her wits' end, she had scrawled *The Friendly Bookshop* and gone to bed. The signwriter was due the next day, so she had ten hours to go with it or think of something better. When she woke the next morning no brainwaves had occurred, but when she looked at the piece of paper it didn't seem such a bad choice. After all, what was wrong with wanting your bookshop to be friendly?

In her new spirit of openness, she had informed Maddy of the change the next morning. Maddy had said nothing, but her shoulders stiffened beneath her boat-necked Breton top. The signwriter, when he arrived, had accepted the name without comment, merely asking what sort of lettering she would like. Jemma chose a rounded, reasonably conservative style, and he set up his ladder and got to work.

And now there was no going back, Jemma had worked harder than ever to make sure that The Friendly Bookshop was a success. She created themed window displays with autumn leaves, pumpkins, and books draped in woollen scarves, or wearing bobble hats. She wrote book recommendations on little cards and attached them to the shelves. She opened an online shop, and listed stock there. Lunch hours became a hasty slice of toast and jam at the counter, or a banana eaten on the fly, and dinner was often delivered by Snacking Cross Road, because Jemma had neither the time nor the inclination to cook once she had closed her laptop.

'You look knackered,' said Luke, snapping her back to the present.

'Thank you so much,' said Jemma. *I'm not even sure if it's all worth it.* Her efforts were achieving something – she could see that from her accounts – but while the shop was now making as much as it had when she took it over, she couldn't help reflecting that it would have been much less bother to put her feet up and let Maddy step into Brian's shoes. She stretched her arms above her head and felt her shoulders click. 'How are things at Burns Books?' she asked, more out of politeness than concern.

'That's why I'm here,' said Luke. 'I'm worried.'

Jemma frowned. 'In what way? Is the shop misbehaving?'

'No, the shop's fine.' Luke pushed his hair back and Jemma noticed that he was rather pale. Of course; he had left the shop in broad daylight to visit her.

'You'd better tell me,' she said. 'Would you mind if I

made a cup of tea first?'

They sat at the counter, Jemma with her tea and Luke with his drinks bottle. He took a pull at it before speaking. 'The shop is absolutely fine. Business is great: books are flying off the shelves. No, it's Raphael. He doesn't seem himself. For one thing, I haven't seen much of him.'

'That's hardly unusual,' Jemma commented.

'But he isn't out buying books or sneaking into Rolando's. He's upstairs in his flat. I don't know what he's doing up there, but when he does come downstairs he looks worried. I've tried asking if he's OK, but he just brushes me off and goes out. I'd follow him, but obviously I can't leave the shop.' His eyes darted around guiltily. 'I shouldn't be here now, but I asked Carl to mind the till upstairs for a few minutes while I came to see you. Raphael went out at eleven, and he hadn't returned by the time I left. I checked Rolando's, but he wasn't there.'

'What does Carl think?' asked Jemma.

Luke stared. 'Don't you know?'

'We've barely seen each other,' said Jemma. 'He's been busy with his play, I've been busy here, and our phones are playing up.'

'Well, he's downstairs, so he doesn't see as much of Raphael anyway,' said Luke. 'But he agrees he isn't his usual self.' He paused. 'Could you come and talk to Raphael when Maddy returns from lunch? He's more likely to tell you.'

Jemma's first impulse was to say no, she couldn't possibly, she was far too busy with running her own place. Then all the support that Raphael had given her rushed in like a determined wave. 'Of course I will,' she said. 'I don't know if it will do any good, but I'll pop down as soon as Maddy gets back. Maybe I can loosen his tongue.'

'I hope so,' said Luke. 'It will be nice to see you in the shop for a change. You've been quite a stranger this last week.'

'I know,' said Jemma. She sighed. 'I'm starting to think running my own bookshop isn't as easy as I thought it would be.'

'It looks great,' said Luke. 'And I like the new name. It does seem a lot friendlier.'

'Despite Maddy's best efforts,' said Jemma. She had done her best to be nice to Maddy and make her feel appreciated, but her behaviour varied with the weather. Some days she was willing and helpful; others she was uncommunicative and sulky. It didn't seem to relate to the books she sold, the customers who came in, or anything in particular. Jemma had been forced to conclude that she was moody and a bit unpredictable.

'I'm sure it'll all work out,' said Luke, and Jemma recognised his tone as a soothing one. 'I really had better go. Hope to see you later.' And with that he whisked through the door, wincing as he stepped over the threshold.

***

In the end, Jemma didn't leave The Friendly Bookshop until nearly two o'clock. Maddy had taken her full lunch hour, which of course she was perfectly entitled to do, but Jemma couldn't help thinking that it was typical of her to do that when Jemma needed to be somewhere else. Then Jemma had to explain that she was popping out to Burns

107

Books and wasn't sure when she would be back, and leave Maddy a list of things to get on with, since she had found herself unable to concentrate for wondering about Raphael. And as Jemma was winding that up she had realised how hungry she was, and nipped upstairs for a fortifying helping of cheese on toast. It wasn't that she was delaying her visit; more that she wanted to be fully prepared for any eventuality.

Perhaps he's worried about another challenge, she thought, as she hurried down Charing Cross Road. *Maybe he's going out and researching books. Or maybe he is going on book-buying trips, and he hasn't mentioned it to Luke.*

She pushed open the door of Burns Books and found Luke at the till, dealing expertly with a line of customers holding piles of books. He smiled at Jemma before he registered who she was, and then the smile vanished as if someone had wiped it away.

'Is the boss in?' asked Jemma, a cold hand clutching at her heart.

'He's upstairs in his rooms,' said Luke. 'A letter came, and he said he needed time to read it.' The smile reappeared. 'Cash or card, madam?'

Jemma walked towards the back of the shop and knocked at the door which led to Raphael's quarters.

There was no response.

She knocked again. Nothing.

'Raphael?' she called. 'It's me, Jemma.'

Silence.

Then she heard a yowl from upstairs. *Folio*. She tried

the handle of the door, and to her surprise, it opened.

Could it be an anonymous letter? she thought as she climbed the stairs. *A threatening letter, like the ones we got before?* But that had been dealt with, and she was pretty sure that neither of the perpetrators would try that again. Certainly not with Raphael.

At the top of the stairs was another closed door. Jemma knocked. 'Raphael, it's Jemma. I've come to see you.'

He is there, isn't he? Then something worse occurred to her. *He hasn't . . . done anything?*

Folio yowled and scratched at the door. Jemma swallowed the hard lump of terror that had lodged in her throat, and opened it.

Inside, it was dark. All the curtains were drawn. Folio rubbed against her shin and meowed, and she reached down carefully to stroke him. He seemed the same size as usual, but his fur was a mess of tangles and burrs. 'Poor Folio,' she said, and Folio purred in agreement.

'Is Raphael here?' she asked the cat.

Folio answered with a short meow and dashed towards the left-hand door, which Jemma was pretty sure led to Raphael's sitting room, though she had never actually been upstairs. She knocked, then entered.

Jemma didn't often think about how Raphael lived, but if ever she did, she imagined good-quality furnishings worn with age, possibly with an air of decayed grandeur. Once her eyes had grown accustomed to the dim room, she saw that if anything, it was spartan. A threadbare high-backed armchair; a small side table with a reading lamp; an old-style television on a rickety-looking unit. The floorboards were covered with a large, worn rug. The most luxurious thing about the room was the wall of shelves that faced her, filled with books and occasional devices which looked as if they might well be either magical, dangerous, or both.

But the focal point of the room was Raphael. He was sitting in the armchair, one hand supporting his forehead, the other clutching a letter with what looked like an official seal at the top. His eyes were squeezed tight shut. Folio hopped onto the other arm of the chair and butted Raphael's arm, but he didn't seem to notice.

'Raphael, what's up?' Jemma advanced into the room, then crouched beside the armchair. 'Is there anything I can do to help?'

Folio meowed again and rubbed his head on Raphael's upper arm. And Raphael ignored him. Jemma had never, ever, seen him fail to respond to Folio.

Suddenly she had an idea. 'I'll be back in a moment,' she said, and ran first down to the ground floor, then to the lower bookshop, where Carl was leaning against the café counter, enjoying a brief lull in customers.

'A double espresso and a cinnamon roll please, as quickly as you can,' she said.

Carl raised his eyebrows.

'Don't ask questions,' Jemma said. 'It's urgent. This could be a matter of life and death.'

Once she was equipped, Jemma hurried back up to Raphael and shoved the coffee and the cinnamon roll under his nose. He sniffed, then an eye opened and swivelled round to the cinnamon roll. 'Is that for me?' he asked.

'Of course it is,' said Jemma. 'Please, Raphael, tell me what's wrong.'

'You can read it for yourself,' he said, and reached out his free hand for the coffee. Jemma relieved him of the letter and replaced it with the cinnamon roll, which he looked at with curiosity, as if he ought to know what to do with it.

Jemma skimmed the letter. The text beneath the seal said *From the European Head of the Keepers' Guild.* Words and phrases jumped out at her:

Following several complaints...

...unbecoming conduct...

...neglect of duty...

...failure to manage effectively...

...formal written warning...

Jemma looked up from the letter. 'What does it mean?' she said. 'I can tell it isn't good, but what is it saying?'

A bark of something like laughter erupted from Raphael. 'What it means, Jemma, is that I've been reprimanded by my boss. What that means, in layperson's terms, is that it's over. It's all over.'

Chapter 14

'Over? What do you mean, over?' Sick dread filled the pit of Jemma's stomach. Whatever the answer was, she didn't think she would like it.

'I shouldn't be sad,' said Raphael. 'I've had a good run. Two hundred years is quite something, when you think about it.'

'But the letter says it's a warning,' said Jemma.

Raphael looked up, then downed half of his espresso in one go. 'I know it says that, but in practice, once you've had a warning, that's it. Your card is marked. You're on borrowed time.'

'But I don't understand this letter,' said Jemma. 'What unbecoming conduct, exactly?'

'That's not so much me as the others,' said Raphael. 'The accusation is that I haven't been sufficiently in control of them.' The corner of his mouth twisted in a wry smile.

'It isn't exactly a fair system, but it's what we're used to.'

Jemma blinked. She had a horrible feeling that her push for equal opportunities and better employment rights had directly caused Raphael's warning, not to mention the anger and resentment of the people it was meant to help. 'It's all gone so very wrong,' she murmured, and buried her head in her hands. She felt if she were in a black hole of despair, and wanted nothing more than to be buried in it and left alone. *This is my fault. I thought I was helping, but obviously not. I didn't even understand what I was dealing with.*

A few moments later a tentative hand touched her shoulder. 'It's not the end of the world,' said Raphael. 'I'm sure there are other things I could do. I mean, I could just run the bookshop. It could be a sort of retirement.'

Jemma removed her hands and stared at him. 'But – but you'd *die*,' she said.

'Most people do,' said Raphael. 'That wouldn't happen immediately. At least, I hope not.'

'No,' said Jemma, looking about her as if she might spot something in the room that could help. 'There has to be a way. There has to.'

'I don't think there is,' said Raphael. Then he sighed. 'I must admit that I didn't expect the reaction I got. Dissent or disagreement, perhaps, but not such anger. I did indicate that I was happy to discuss the matter, but not one person has taken me up on that.' He ran a hand through his hair. 'I should probably prepare for a challenge. That will be the next thing.'

'Well, it shouldn't be,' said Jemma. 'The system

shouldn't work like that.'

'Ah, but it does,' said Raphael, and bit into his cinnamon roll for consolation.

'I'll try and think of something,' said Jemma. 'I'll do whatever I can to help. This is my fault, and if I can fix it, I will.'

Raphael patted her arm. 'I do appreciate it, Jemma, but I'm not sure what you can do. I don't mean that as a slight, not at all; I don't see what anybody could do.'

Jemma sensed the conversation could go round in circles for hours if she let it. 'I'm going back to my shop,' she said. 'But I'll keep thinking about it, and if I have any ideas I'll be in touch.' She got up and studied him. 'Are you sure you'll be all right?'

'Of course,' said Raphael. 'Folio is here.' He tickled the cat under the chin and received a purr in return. 'I'll go downstairs in a bit and look after the ground floor. It'll probably do me good to think about something else.'

'I think you're right,' said Jemma. 'One of the customers might give you an idea. Or maybe a book. I'm sure I saw some employment law textbooks—'

Raphael laughed. 'I'm no expert on employment law, but I'd hazard a guess that the Keepers' Guild runs on an entirely different legal system,' he said. 'Anyway, you get back to your bookshop. Books to sell, people to serve.'

Luke raised his eyebrows when Jemma emerged into the main shop, but she shook her head. It was too big and too horrible to explain. 'I'll do the best I can to help,' she said. 'Hopefully I'll have a brainwave.'

'I hope you do,' said Luke. 'I miss Raphael, you know.

While he's not in the shop that much, at the moment he's not here in a completely different way.'

Jemma nodded, and the tinkle of the shop bell as she left sounded like a death knell.

***

Jemma's feet dragged as she walked down Charing Cross Road to The Friendly Bookshop. When she arrived, though, she found it looking far from friendly. The window was completely empty, the spotlight shining on an absence.

'What's going on?' she said, as she opened the door.

Maddy stood behind the counter, packing books into a box. The former window display, if Jemma wasn't mistaken.

'What on earth are you doing?' A couple of customers were browsing, but Jemma had reached the point where she didn't care what the customers thought. 'Why are there no books in the window?' Then she saw that the shelves at the front of the shop, the shelves she had filled with her lovely new books, were also completely bare.

'It isn't working,' said Maddy. 'The fiction isn't working.'

'Yes it is,' said Jemma. 'We're selling more books, and making the same money as the bookshop did before.'

'But what about the expense?' said Maddy. 'What about the cost of all those books, and the redecoration? I doubt you've taken *that* into account. I suspect you've been looking at the profits and ignoring the costs.'

'Don't be ridiculous,' snapped Jemma, and a woman nearby, flicking through *A Brief History of Time*, jumped. 'I've lost count of how often you've made changes without asking me first, and as far as I'm concerned, this is the last time.'

Maddy came out from behind the counter and faced her. She stood tall, and two spots of colour burned on her cheekbones. 'And what will you do, exactly?'

The words *Fire you* were on Jemma's lips, but she couldn't bring herself to say them. What if she were in the wrong and Maddy sued her for unfair dismissal? Or what if she went through the accounts and found that Maddy was right, and she *had* overspent, and she had made a mess of things yet again? But she drew herself up too and glared at Maddy. 'I'm sending you home,' she said. 'I'm not prepared to tolerate an employee who constantly undermines me. I suggest you think about that before you come in tomorrow. *If* you do.'

Maddy flung up her chin. 'I shall most certainly think that over,' she said. She pushed the box of books away from her as if it were contaminated, got her bag and coat, and clumped out of the shop.

Jemma exhaled, closed her eyes, and pinched the bridge of her nose. When she opened her eyes she found that everyone left in the shop was staring at her.

'But isn't *she* the manager?' said the woman who had jumped earlier, laying her book on the counter. 'I thought she was.'

'No, she isn't,' said Jemma, 'but she clearly thinks she is.' She processed the sale, then opened the box of books on the counter and began putting them back in the window, possibly with less than her usual care. 'If any of you were looking for fiction,' she said, when she had finished, 'tell me what you'd like and I'll check on the database. It appears that while I was in a meeting with the owner, my assistant has taken it upon herself to rearrange the shop.' The customers stared. 'Do carry on,' she said. 'Don't mind me.'

Jemma found her books boxed neatly and stacked in the far corner of the stockroom. *I trusted her alone for what, an hour, and look what happened.* Re-shelving the books ought to have been restful and calming, but Jemma found herself pushing them firmly into their places on the shelf in a way that she wished she could do with Maddy. *What is wrong with her? Why won't she accept my authority? Is there something wrong with me? Am I a bad manager?*

By the time the shop closed for the day, though she had fully restocked the shelves and even sold a reasonable amount of books, Jemma was thoroughly convinced that she was, quite possibly, the worst bookshop manager in the entire world. *So much for helping Raphael,* she thought, as she locked the shop door, set the alarm, and stomped upstairs to her flat. *I'm a complete failure. Everything I touch turns to crap.* She kept up a constant stream of angry muttering as she slammed around the flat, turning the TV up loud enough to give herself a headache, breaking the teabag as she made a drink, and, devastatingly, discovering that she was out of emergency biscuits. That was when she broke down in tears and huddled in the corner of the sofa, rocking and worrying about Raphael, and the terrible things she had done.

Chapter 15

After a while Jemma's sniffling got on her own nerves, so she surfed mindlessly between channels, staring at local news, then a brightly coloured cartoon, then a consumer programme, then a house-renovation show. She didn't care about any of it; she just felt numb. *There's nothing left.*

She could hear someone knocking at the door downstairs: three light taps, a pause, then persistent, harder knocking. Whoever it was, she didn't want to know. Then a voice shouted 'Jemma! Jemma, are you there?'

It was Carl's voice.

Jemma debated whether or not to let him in. On one hand, she didn't feel like talking to anybody. On the other, it was Carl, and she hadn't seen him for days. Then her phone solved the problem by ringing. She glanced at the display: *Mum.*

'I'm coming,' she yelled, opened the door of the flat,

and clattered downstairs.

Carl looked rather confused when he saw her face. 'What's up?'

Jemma shrugged. 'Everything.' She felt as if that ought to be her cue to weep on his shoulder, but it seemed pointless.

'Can I come up? Or would you rather come out?'

Jemma eyed him. He was still in his barista uniform of black polo shirt and jeans. 'Aren't you supposed to be rehearsing?'

Carl exhaled, and seemed to deflate in the process. 'I was worried about you,' he said. 'Luke told me that you'd been in and spoken to Raphael, and that you wouldn't tell him what was wrong. And you didn't come and see me.'

'I had to get back to the shop,' said Jemma. 'And when I did, I found that Maddy had rearranged everything again, so I sent her home for the day.' She leaned on the doorframe, looking at him. 'You can come up if you like, but I'm not sure why you'd want to. I'm not very good company right now.' She led the way upstairs. *In fact, I probably haven't been good company for weeks.* A shiver came out of nowhere. 'You haven't come round to dump me, have you?' She said it lightly, but kept climbing the stairs, not wanting to turn and see his face.

Carl said nothing, but she heard his feet behind her. A part of her wanted to press him for an answer – *You have, haven't you?* – while she also wanted to kick herself for potentially putting the idea into his head. She reached the landing and waved her hand at the sitting room. 'Would you like a drink?'

'I want to talk to you,' said Carl. 'I'm not happy with the way things are at the moment. Before you say anything, that doesn't mean I want to break up with you. But we aren't really going out at the moment, are we? We don't text because of the weird phone thing, and you're too busy to meet up after work, and I'm busy with rehearsals now we've scheduled the shows—'

'Wait a minute,' said Jemma. 'You're putting on the play?'

'Yes,' said Carl. 'Raphael said we could put on a couple of performances downstairs at the end of November.' He walked into the sitting room and sat on the sofa. 'I would have told you, but—'

'I know, there wasn't an opportunity,' said Jemma. She remembered when she and Raphael had discovered the crypt in the basement, and her suggestion that they could put on events. *They've done it without me.* 'I'm sorry, but everything's been so busy.'

'Everything is always so busy,' said Carl.

'Yes, but this is different,' said Jemma. 'Maddy is undermining me at every turn, and that's nothing compared to what's going on with Raphael—' She clapped a hand over her mouth.

Carl stared at her. 'What's going on with Raphael?'

Jemma sighed, walked into the sitting room, and flopped in the opposite corner of the sofa. She looked at Carl. 'He could lose his job,' she said. 'His boss has given him a warning.'

'He's got a boss?'

Jemma nodded. Then, judging that she might as well let

the whole cat out of the bag, she told him the rest of it.

'That's bizarre,' said Carl. 'Why would people want their jobs to be insecure? Why wouldn't they want better terms and conditions? Obviously they're not in any sort of union – or if they are, it's the strangest one I ever heard of.'

'I can't get my head round it either,' said Jemma. 'Apparently people have been complaining over Raphael's head. They must think that will do them some good, and apparently it has.' She frowned. 'Maybe Raphael's boss wants a quiet life and he doesn't care who's right.'

'Maybe,' said Carl. 'What's going on with Maddy? I thought you two were getting on better.'

'We were,' said Jemma. 'Then we weren't again, and I don't know why. I thought maybe she was just moody, but sometimes it feels as if she is – almost a different person.'

'Do you think… Not that I know anything about this, but could she have some sort of personality disorder?'

'If she has,' said Jemma, 'it's come on very recently; Raphael has never mentioned anything. And Brian wouldn't have put up with it. I'd like to have seen his face if Maddy started moving his displays around and telling him that things weren't working.'

'True,' said Carl. 'She'd get her marching orders.' He studied Jemma. 'So why do you think she's doing it with you?'

'Maybe she thinks she can get away with it,' said Jemma. 'Maybe she thinks I'm a pushover. Or maybe I just really, really wind her up, and she can't stop herself. But afterwards, she's so very sorry. Sometimes I call her out over something, and she apologises, and she's even helpful.

I mean, more than she needs to be. For all I know, she'll come in tomorrow morning and be full of apologies and nice as pie, then rearrange everything after lunch.'

Carl leaned over and touched her arm. 'Would you fire her?'

Jemma considered the question. 'Not without speaking to Raphael first, and I don't want to bother him right now. He's got enough going on, never mind me coming to him with personnel issues.' She giggled at the idea of knocking on Raphael's door to request employment law advice. Then she found that she couldn't stop.

Carl gave her a sharp look. 'Stop that, Jemma,' he said, quietly and firmly.

Jemma, shocked, stopped immediately. 'Thank you,' she said. 'I don't know why I did that.'

He shuffled along the sofa and put an arm round her. 'You're worried and upset,' he said. He gave her a squeeze. 'I don't like seeing you like this, Jemma, but I don't know what to do. I'm not even sure I can help you.' His hold loosened, and he looked away. 'I feel a bit useless.'

'Don't be daft, of course you're not useless,' said Jemma. 'Talking to you is helping, it really is.' She smiled. 'And you turning up meant I could ignore a phone call from my mum.'

'Oh, so I'm the slightly better option, am I?' said Carl. Then he grinned. 'Well, if I helped…' Then he grew serious. 'Why didn't you want to talk to your mum?'

'Oh, nothing's ever right,' said Jemma. 'If it isn't perfect, then it wasn't good enough. If it is perfect, then I'm either aiming too low or doing the wrong thing.

Anyway. Do you want a drink?'

'I wouldn't mind,' said Carl. 'I take it you don't want to go for a bite to eat.'

'I know it's unlike me to be uninterested in food,' said Jemma, 'but I'm not that fussed.' Carl was scrutinising her. 'Why are you looking at me like that?'

'When did you last cook a meal?' he said. 'I mean properly, from scratch. Not putting something in the microwave, or doing pasta with a jar of sauce. Not that there's anything wrong with that,' he added.

She frowned. 'Why do you want to know?'

'I'm not sure,' he said. 'It seems important, somehow.'

Jemma thought. Not that week – that had mostly been toast, occasionally cheese on toast, and at least one pizza. She couldn't really answer for the week before, either. 'I'm not entirely sure,' she admitted. Then she grimaced. 'That isn't good, is it?'

'It isn't like you,' said Carl. 'I remember when I brought you home that first time, and we went out to lunch, and you were talking about how you'd started cooking and you were really into it.'

'It's not that I've gone off it or anything,' said Jemma. 'I've just been busy.'

'But you're often busy,' said Carl. 'And it hasn't stopped you cooking before. In fact, you said you found it relaxing. So why don't you cook now?'

Jemma thought – or tried to think, because nothing came to mind. She could remember cooking, certainly, and enjoying it. But somehow it seemed as if someone else had done that, a long time ago, not her. And the idea of finding a recipe, assembling ingredients, and methodically working through the steps to produce a meal seemed very remote indeed. 'I don't know,' she said, in a small, uncertain voice.

'I wonder…' said Carl. 'Tell me what Raphael was like when you went up to his flat.'

'But I already said—'

'Humour me.'

Jemma's brow furrowed. 'He was sitting in the armchair with his head in his hand, clutching the letter. He didn't answer me when I called him, and he didn't pay any attention to Folio.' She looked at Carl. 'I managed to bring him round with a cinnamon roll, but even then…'

'And Maddy's behaving oddly, and you – well, something's stopping you from doing things you'd normally do, like cooking—'

'I'm so tired,' said Jemma. 'And Raphael's had all this bother to deal with. It's no wonder he isn't himself—'

'There it is again,' said Carl. '*Not himself. Sometimes she seems like a different person.* And you aren't yourself, either.'

A chill ran down Jemma's spine. 'What do you mean?'

'I'm not entirely sure,' said Carl. 'But something's going on with all three of you, and I intend to get to the bottom of it.' He paused, his face set and determined. 'You know what?'

'What?'

'A cup of tea would really help.'

Chapter 16

The next day Jemma was in the bookshop by eight o'clock, waiting to see which Maddy would come in. Despite a long chat with Carl the previous evening, they had come up with no better plan of action than keeping their eyes open and, if possible, teasing more information out of Raphael and Maddy.

Jemma got her answer when she heard a tap at the door at twenty-five minutes past eight, and Maddy shuffled in, thoroughly hangdog. 'I'll understand if you tell me to go away,' she said. 'I don't know what came over me.'

'Neither do I,' said Jemma. 'And we should discuss it.'

Maddy winced. 'Could I apologise, and then we can draw a line under it?'

'We've tried that,' said Jemma. 'Everything is fine for a few days, but the minute I leave the shop you start messing around again.' She wanted to look Maddy in the eye, but

Maddy wasn't letting her, keeping her gaze firmly on her twisting hands. 'Why do you do it, Maddy? You must know all that happens is that I get cross with you and put it back as it was.'

'I do know,' said Maddy. 'I – I suppose I'm not as ready for change as I thought I was.'

'I'm sure you've said that before,' said Jemma. 'But why keep doing something if you know it doesn't work?'

Maddy said nothing, peeping at Jemma from under her eyelashes.

'Maddy, you would let me know if you were feeling ill, wouldn't you?' said Jemma.

'I'm perfectly well, thank you,' said Maddy, looking Jemma full in the face for the first time. 'There is absolutely nothing wrong with me.'

'Good,' said Jemma. 'I'm glad to hear it.'

'I haven't had a day off sick in ten years,' Maddy continued. 'That's how long I've been working here.'

'That's a long time,' said Jemma. 'What did you do before?'

The corner of Maddy's mouth moved upwards a tiny bit. 'I worked in an antiquarian bookshop just down the road. But I'd always been interested in this shop – I used to pop over in my lunch hour – and when a job came up—'

'I see,' said Jemma. 'So antiquarian books are in your blood, sort of.'

Maddy actually giggled. 'I suppose they are.'

The letterbox rattled, and a few envelopes dropped onto the mat. 'Post's here,' said Jemma, walking to the door. Out of the corner of her eye she caught a quick, nervous glance from Maddy, whose expression seemed to have frozen. She flicked through the pile. 'Utility bill . . . letter . . . might be a card . . . oh, and one for you.' She passed it to Maddy. 'You'll have to let your correspondent know we've had a name change.'

'Thank you,' said Maddy, taking the letter and thrusting it into her bag unopened. 'Yes, I shall.'

'It must be nice to get a personal letter,' said Jemma. 'Handwritten, too. I don't think I've ever seen ink that colour.'

'Isn't it your morning to go to Burns Books?' said Maddy. 'Not that I'm trying to get rid of you—'

'Yes, it is,' said Jemma. She gave Maddy what she hoped was a moderately stern look. 'Can I trust you not to do anything to the shop while I'm gone?'

Maddy gazed past Jemma, a faraway expression on her face.

'Maddy?'

Maddy snapped to attention. 'Everything will be fine,' she said.

'Good,' said Jemma. 'Then I'll head out. The till's primed, and we have plenty of bags. If anything happens, you can always phone me at the shop.' She frowned. *Why did I say that?*

'Yes, Jemma,' said Maddy.

Jemma got her coat, slung her bag over her shoulder, and left. She had gone a few steps when she realised she hadn't turned the shop sign round. She was about to open the door and do it when she glimpsed Maddy, standing where Jemma had left her, devouring the letter which had arrived a few minutes before.

Whatever, thought Jemma, and hurried away.

***

She was startled to find Raphael on the ground floor of the bookshop, dressed in a conventional dark-blue suit with a white shirt and red bow tie, humming to himself as he fed the till with bank bags of change. Folio sat on the counter, supervising the process and occasionally patting an empty bag. 'Hello,' said Jemma. 'You look happier, if you don't mind me saying.'

'I am,' said Raphael. 'I've decided on a course of action, and you can help.'

'Oh good,' said Jemma. 'I think. What would you like me to do?'

'I'm calling a meeting,' Raphael replied. 'Actually, I've already called it and sent the invitations.'

'Gosh,' said Jemma. 'That's . . . dynamic. Who have you invited?'

'Everyone,' said Raphael. 'Well, not everyone, but all my staff and associates. And if you wouldn't mind, I'd like you to explain how you influenced the recruitment process.'

'I see,' said Jemma, quailing inwardly. 'Um, when is it?'

'Ten o'clock,' said Raphael.

'*Today?*'

'Yes, today. Seize the day. Strike while the iron is hot. Seize the opportunity with both hands – well, as long as it isn't a hot iron. You get my drift.'

Jemma gazed at Raphael, bewildered. On one hand, the

thought of addressing a meeting full of strangers was terrifying. On the other, Raphael seemed more enthusiastic than he had for a long time, and utterly convinced that his plan would work. 'Where will the meeting be?' she asked. 'Are you closing the bookshop?'

'No need,' said Raphael. 'We can do it upstairs.'

'What?'

'It's a virtual meeting,' said Raphael, as if speaking to a small child. 'We can do it on my laptop.'

'You have a laptop?'

'Of course I— Um, yes, I do,' said Raphael. 'Though I don't use it often.'

'I figured,' said Jemma. *All this time I thought he was a complete technophobe, and here he is running a virtual meeting*. She remembered all the times she had scrolled slowly through spreadsheets for him and explained formulas. 'I suppose you emailed the invites?'

'Oh yes,' said Raphael. 'I sent a brief agenda to my mailing list.'

'Good grief,' said Jemma. 'Would you mind if I put the kettle on? I have a sudden urge for tea.'

'What a good idea,' said Raphael. 'In fact, I'll put the kettle on, and you can go and say hello to Luke and Carl.'

Jemma descended the stairs slowly, her mind whirling. *Whatever next*, she thought. *In fact, I don't want to know.*

'How's it going?' they both said in a ragged chorus, as she pushed open the great oak door.

'Fine, I think,' she said.

'Raphael seems happy today,' said Carl, in an encouraging voice.

'Yes, he does,' Jemma replied. 'Luke, you'll be on the upstairs till this morning. Raphael and I will be busy.'

'Uh-huh,' said Luke.

Jemma looked at him more closely. Luke was back in head-to-toe black, his hair straggling from under his beanie hat, and he hadn't shaved that morning. 'How are you?' she asked.

'Oh, fine,' said Luke, continuing to look glum. 'Well, no, not really. I've been ghosted.' He sighed. 'If she didn't want to see me again, she could've texted. Although come to think of it, I'm not sure she can.'

'I'm not even going to ask,' said Jemma. 'But I'm sorry.'

'It's OK,' said Luke. 'We were a bit of an odd couple anyway. And we only went out twice. Better now than later, I guess.'

'How was Maddy?' Carl asked.

'Apologetic,' said Jemma. 'We had a chat. She's promised not to change the shop around while I'm gone. I'll have to trust her, otherwise I won't be able to go anywhere. Anyway, she was reading a letter when I left. Hopefully that will take her mind off making changes.'

'Jemma!' called Raphael. 'Tea's ready.'

'That's my cue,' said Jemma. 'Hopefully I'll see you guys later and we can catch up properly.' She surveyed the lower floor of the shop, which was in impeccable order yet still managed to look cosy. *I wish I could come down here and read*, she thought. *A good book, and a cappuccino, and maybe Folio next to me.* The pull was so strong that she took a step towards the nearest armchair before shaking the thought off and galloping upstairs.

***

'Are you ready?' said Raphael, at five minutes to ten.

'I think so.' Jemma had already visited the staff bathroom to brush her hair and put lipstick on. She flicked through the bullet points she had scribbled on a couple of index cards, muttering them to herself. 'Do you promise I won't have to talk for more than five minutes?'

'And take questions,' said Raphael, in a reasonable tone. He had fetched an extra chair and placed it beside the armchair, and put the little table in front of both. 'Time to set up.' He went to a corner cupboard that Jemma hadn't noticed, opened it, and brought out a laptop. A slim, impressive-looking laptop.

'You are full of surprises, Raphael Burns,' said Jemma, as he opened it and began clicking on icons.

'Here we go.' A window opened, and in the middle was a countdown clock captioned *Time to Meeting*. 'Webcam on.' He clicked and their faces filled the screen.

'Do I really look that pale?' said Jemma, eyeing herself with distaste.

'Yes,' said Raphael. 'You need to get out more. Now, I'll keep the sound off until people start joining. I've had a few apologies, but I'm expecting around a hundred and fifty people to show up.'

'A hundred and fifty?' Jemma blurted. 'You didn't mention that.'

'Oh, and I'm recording it,' said Raphael. 'That way I can send the meeting to everyone who missed it.'

'Ugh.' Jemma slumped in her chair.

'They can see you, you know,' said Raphael, waving a hand at the screen. Jemma saw two impassive faces sharing the screen with them, sat up straight, and stuck a smile on her face. 'I'm *so* going to get you back for this, Raphael,' she said, out of the side of her mouth.

More and more faces popped up. 'Interesting,' commented Raphael. 'Most of the people here so far are pretty moderate. I was expecting the rabble-rousers to turn up early, to psych me out. If and when they join, I'll point them out to you.'

'Thank you so much,' said Jemma.

'One minute,' said Raphael. 'Sound on.' He waved at the camera, and a few hands waved back.

Jemma crossed her fingers. 'Good luck,' she whispered. The clock ticked down.

'Right, good morning everyone,' said Raphael. 'I expect you're wondering why I've called this meeting today, although those of you who were present at our last update will no doubt have a good idea.'

Two more faces appeared on the screen. 'Ah, good morning,' said Raphael. 'We've just started, so you haven't missed anything.' He glanced at Jemma, then pointed at the faces in the two new windows.

Jemma gasped. *It's them!* She nudged Raphael, who ignored her. 'So if we're all quite ready,' he said, pointedly not looking at the two latecomers, 'let's begin.'

Chapter 17

Jemma did her best to keep a smile on her face as her brain worked furiously. *It is them, isn't it?* She leaned forward slightly to examine their two windows. She remembered those blonde highlights, the tailored designer outfit, the icy demeanour. And she recognised both De Vere's tweed jacket and his superciliousness. *I'm absolutely sure of it. But what can I do?*

She tuned into what Raphael was saying. 'Some of you may be surprised to hear that I received a letter from Armand Dupont, the European Head of the Guild. It was not a pleasant letter, and he indicated that he had received complaints about me. No one has contacted me to discuss the proposed recruitment changes. I was not so foolish as to assume that meant you were all happy, but I hoped that you would seek a meeting rather than go over my head.'

Even in the tiny window, Jemma saw the posh woman's

nostrils flare, while Mr De Vere appeared to be looking down his nose from a great height.

'At the last meeting there was an – atmosphere, and a few people dominated the discussion,' said Raphael. 'Indeed, some of you tried to talk over me. I explained that my change of heart regarding our recruitment process was based on feedback from a potential candidate. However, I'm not sure many of you heard.'

Angry buzzing came from the screen, like a colony of wasps about to strike.

'So I have invited my contact to speak to you herself.' Raphael turned to Jemma.

'And what credentials does she have?' demanded an exceedingly well-bred voice.

'The same as all of us, Drusilla,' Raphael replied. 'Experience and knowledge, though in a somewhat different field. I'll mute everybody so that Jemma can speak.'

Jemma picked up her index cards. She felt as if she ought to stand, but that was impossible. She also felt desperate for a glass of water. She swallowed, looked at the tessellation of faces, and tried to smile. 'Hello everyone,' she said. *Don't wave. Whatever you do, don't wave.* She could actually feel her hand lifting. She grabbed her wrist with the other hand, and forced it down.

'My name is Jemma James, and until a few months ago I had no idea such a thing as the Keepers' Guild existed.' *I can imagine what they're thinking.*

'While working at Burns Books, and managing The Friendly Bookshop, I have gained experience. However, before joining the bookshop I worked as an analyst, and I have a keen interest in management theory and business strategy. Your current recruitment model encourages you to attack your colleagues to gain promotion, or defend your own position against attack. At any moment your job and your home could be in jeopardy; that isn't a healthy way to live. I'm sure some of you don't want change. But talented people who don't want to take such an unstable job will either leave the Guild, or never join it.'

She glanced at Raphael. 'Go on, Jemma,' he said.

'Raphael invited me to apply for the position of Assistant Keeper; however, I could not consider it. For people with families and caring responsibilities, the risk of having either to leave them, or move everyone to a new area without a job to fund it, isn't worth taking.' Jemma paused, saw no obvious hostility on the faces before her, and ploughed on.

'If no new people come into your organisation, eventually no new thoughts will enter the organisation either, and it will grow stale. Then how will you perform your great task of preserving, managing, and protecting knowledge? The threats out there may change, but what if you can't?'

She considered stopping there, but it seemed a very negative way to leave things.

'I don't want to sound negative,' she said hastily. 'But what a way to spend your working life; either plotting to overthrow your colleagues, or watching your juniors for signs of aggression. Wouldn't it be better if you could concentrate on your work, instead of having that constant distraction? And wouldn't you rather enjoy your home life without worrying that it could be taken away from you in an instant?'

She gathered herself for a conclusion. 'I hope that what I have said makes sense, and I urge you to consider it, both for yourselves and for the future of the Guild. Thank you.'

Raphael smiled at her. 'Well said, Jemma. Does anyone have a question? If so, please raise your hand, either by pushing the button or by the antiquated method of actually moving your arm, and I'll unmute you one at a time.'

Please don't unmute those two, Jemma thought. *At least, not yet.*

'Percy, I see your hand is up,' said Raphael, and reached towards the trackpad. Jemma crossed her fingers.

One of the squares filled the screen, and she recognised the elderly man with a monocle who had bought *Jane Eyre*.

'I enjoyed your speech, Jemma, though it doesn't apply to me,' he said. 'I am an old man, and I have no plans to take over the world.' He chortled at his own joke. 'Where was I? Oh yes. Based as I am in a suburban backwater, I doubt any young thrusting individuals will challenge me any time soon. Yet I am not getting any younger, even if I am getting no older.' He bestowed a beatific smile on his listeners.

'One day in the not too distant future, I may wish to relinquish my position and retire. I am not particularly keen on the idea of watching a gaggle of aspiring Assistant Keepers fighting over my role as if they were dogs scrapping for a bone; I would like my replacement to be appointed with dignity. And that is how I wish to leave my position, rather than fearing I shall be thrust out of my library and made to leave the place I have called home for so long. I have seen the changes Jemma is making at her bookshop, and I for one am in favour of them. We need to move with the times.'

'Thank you, Percy; those were relevant and heartfelt words,' said Raphael. He nudged Jemma, and pointed to the chat window at the side of the display. It was scrolling quickly. Jemma saw comments like *Good point*, and *Yes, what am I supposed to do with the children?* and *This sounds too good to be true*. She sighed. Of course, you had to accept some scepticism.

'Ah, Drusilla, I thought you might have something to say.' Raphael reached towards the trackpad and the blonde woman's face filled the screen. She was almost all glare.

'Thank you so much for your speech, my dear,' she said. 'Would you mind telling me how many years you worked as an analyst?'

OK, thought Jemma. *I can handle this.* 'After graduating I joined a management training scheme, where I both worked and learnt management and analytical skills,' she said. 'I was in the scheme for two years, then transitioned into a full-time analytical role which I held for two more years.'

'So, four years then,' said Drusilla. 'If we're feeling generous.' She paused just long enough for Jemma to feel that she ought to respond, then continued. 'You do realise, dear, that most of us have been part of the Keepers' Guild for well over a hundred years. What you're proposing is nothing more than a passing fad.'

'What about equal rights?' said Jemma. 'What about human rights, in fact?'

Drusilla said nothing, merely looking amused. 'Really, this is like any occupation,' she said. 'There is work to be done, and occasionally, sacrifices to be made. The organisation is paramount. I'm sure that your keen business intelligence would be in agreement with that.'

'Actually, no,' said Jemma. 'Research shows that employees who have a good work-life balance perform better.'

'Oh, research,' scoffed Priscilla. 'You can make numbers do whatever you want. Of course, as an analyst, you know that. You've probably faked statistics in your time.'

'I most certainly have not,' said Jemma. 'And if you have to rely on criticising my youth and resorting to personal attacks, then I don't think your argument is worth much.'

Drusilla recoiled slightly, then recovered her composure and lifted her chin. 'If you can't keep your temper under pressure, dear, then this isn't the career for you.'

Raphael, looking pained, leaned towards the screen. 'Does anyone else have any useful or relevant comments to make?'

Jemma regarded the sea of faces. Comments were still scrolling down the right-hand side of the screen.

I'm not sure I want new people coming in and telling us what to do.

Maybe we should do a six-month trial and monitor it.

Does anyone know when this finishes?

She swallowed, and wished again for a glass of water. *Well, I said my piece, although I have no idea if it was any use.* Then she remembered what she had wanted to tell Raphael. She flipped over an index card and grabbed the pen she had used to make notes. She scribbled: *Drusilla, De Vere and Percy have all visited my shop.* She nudged Raphael and pushed the card towards him. He read it and pursed his lips, considering for a moment.

'I see plenty of comments, but no one appears to have any burning questions. I have delayed advertising the post in the hope of reaching a consensus, but it is not fair to delay further. My door is still open for discussion, and I ask that anyone wishing to speak to me does so by the end of next week. Pending any necessary changes, I aim to recruit a new Assistant Keeper for Westminster by Christmas.' He paused, but no one spoke. 'Speaking of Christmas, we have to finalise this year's festivities. I believe you are leading on this, Nina?'

A small blonde woman with winged glasses and an Alice band took over the screen. 'As ever, we have three choices for this year's theme, and I would like to present them to you.'

Jemma nudged Raphael and pointed to the mute button. He pressed it. 'Can I go and get a drink?' she asked. 'I'm gasping.'

'Of course,' said Raphael.

'A desert island theme would be new, but it doesn't feel very Christmassy…'

'What do you think about' – Jemma mouthed the next

words, even though they were muted – 'those three?' She tapped the index card.

'Interesting,' said Raphael. 'And not unexpected. I know Drusilla and De Vere are friends with Brian. Same university. And no, don't ask me which.'

'Or an Australian beach theme…'

'Percy's a bit of an oddity,' said Raphael. 'A nice oddity, though. And he's impressed with you.'

'And there's always traditional Dickensian, but we've done that so often.'

'I have to talk to you when this meeting finishes,' said Jemma. 'How much more of it is there?'

'Maybe ten, fifteen minutes?'

'So if you type A, B, or C in the chat window, I shall collect your votes and we'll go with the majority.'

Raphael unmuted himself. 'Most concisely done, Nina. Shall we say five minutes to make your decision, then we'll reconvene.' He clicked the mute button. 'Jemma, why don't you see if Carl can rustle up some drinks? I feel the need for a strong coffee.'

A few minutes later they were both supplied with caffeine, and Nina, her mouth turned down, announced the festive result. 'I can't say I'm surprised,' she began. 'Perhaps Desert Island and Australian Beach Christmas were a little too similar; they have scored 31% and 33% of the votes respectively. Three people abstained. Therefore the winning option, yet again, is a Dickensian Christmas celebration with 35% of the vote.'

'Thank you, Nina,' said Raphael. 'That concludes our short agenda, but does anyone have any other business?

Any relevant business, I should add.' He surveyed the sea of faces. 'I see no raised hands. In that case, if you wish to speak to me privately, my door is always open. I shall communicate with you again before I advertise the post, and inform you of any changes. Until then, I hope you have a safe and knowledgeable week.' He beamed at them, and ended the meeting.

He turned to Jemma. 'How do you think that went?'

'It was OK,' said Jemma. 'To be honest, I thought they'd be much meaner to me.'

'You probably surprised a lot of them,' said Raphael. 'They won't be used to hearing views from someone who isn't, so to speak, one of us. I suspect many of them, though they kept quiet, agreed with what you said. It does actually make sense.'

'You're so kind,' said Jemma. She took a gulp of her cappuccino, which she felt she had earned approximately ten times over. 'Anyway, why do you think they came to my shop?'

Raphael considered. 'Did they buy books?'

'Well, yes, but I'm sure they could have got them elsewhere at trade prices.'

'True,' said Raphael. 'In that case, they probably wanted to see what you were doing with Brian's shop. Unless they were checking up on Maddy.'

'Do you think they reported back to Brian?' asked Jemma.

'I wouldn't be surprised,' said Raphael. 'Certainly not in the case of De Vere and Drusilla. Percy may have come out of curiosity. He likes a trip to the city once in a while.'

Report back... Suddenly Jemma's blood ran cold, and the hand holding her cappuccino shook. She put it down before she spilt it on the laptop. 'Maddy was reading a letter when I left,' she said. 'Do you think she's in touch with Brian? Could that explain her behaviour?'

Raphael laughed. 'Maddy is a very sensible woman.' He frowned. 'But what you've described doesn't sound like Maddy. Did you see the letter?'

'It was addressed to Maddy, so I didn't open it,' said Jemma. 'The handwriting was old-fashioned and shaky, and it slanted backwards. I could just make out Maddy's name. But the strangest thing was the colour of the ink.'

'Can you describe it?' asked Raphael.

'Yes, it was blue. Not navy blue, and not electric blue, and not bright blue—'

'Wait a minute.' Raphael opened Google and typed rapidly, then clicked on the first result before Jemma had a chance to read it. The screen loaded, and showed a hexagonal ink bottle of exactly the right colour.

'That's it,' said Jemma. 'Mysterious Blue.' She gazed at Raphael. 'How did you know?'

He rolled his eyes. 'Brian never uses anything else. I should have realised he was up to something, but I never thought he'd move so quickly.'

Jemma turned to him, eyes wide. 'What do you think he's told Maddy to do?'

'I have no idea,' said Raphael. 'But we should go to your bookshop right away, and find out.'

Chapter 18

Jemma scurried down Charing Cross Road alongside Raphael. What might Maddy have done this time? What *could* she have done? She peered ahead. She couldn't see flames or smoke, which was something.

'Jemma, I can feel you worrying,' said Raphael, not breaking stride. 'Please don't.'

'I'm trying,' said Jemma. 'Strangely, my corporate training didn't cover what to do when your deadly rival has put a spy in your shop. There wasn't a module on undercover espionage.'

'Call that an education,' said Raphael. 'Anyway, here we are.' He waved his hand at the shop. 'Things don't seem too bad.'

'Let's wait until we get inside, shall we?' said Jemma, and pushed open the door.

She glanced at the front shelves. As she expected, her

books had been removed and Brian's books, as she thought of them, put in their place. 'What did I say?' she cried.

There was no answer.

'I knew it,' she said to Raphael. 'She's probably messing about in the stockroom right now.' She looked around the shop and spied the letter, lying on the counter. 'There it is!' She sprang across the room and seized it, scanning the lines.

Then she turned to Raphael. 'I don't understand. It's just . . . a letter.' She handed it to him.

'*Dear Maddy*,' Raphael read aloud, '*I hope this letter finds you well—*'

Maddy erupted into the room. 'How did you come– Oh.' She pulled up, staring.

'I begin to see,' said Raphael. He continued to read. '*I am very well, and finding my new surroundings most stimulating.*'

Maddy ran to the front shelves and began removing books, stacking them on the floor.

'*I hope you are upholding the standards of the bookshop while I am away.*'

Maddy jumped to her feet and ran into the stockroom.

Raphael followed her. '*Finding my new surroundings most stimulating,*' he repeated.

Maddy passed him on her way to the shelves, and continued emptying them.

'What's wrong with her?' said Jemma. 'Is she under a spell?'

'In a way,' said Raphael. 'Jemma, call her by her name.'

'Maddy,' said Jemma, 'please stop doing that.'

Maddy's arms dropped to her sides. She turned, saw Jemma, and blinked. 'Hello, Jemma,' she said, uncertainly. 'You haven't been gone long.' Her gaze settled on Raphael. 'You brought Mr Burns.'

'We wondered how you were getting on,' said Raphael, 'so I decided to pay the bookshop a visit. Maddy, would you mind making tea?'

'Yes, of course, Mr Burns,' said Maddy, and hurried to the back room.

'OK, that's weird,' said Jemma, as soon as Maddy had disappeared. 'What's going on?'

'I'm no expert,' said Raphael, 'but I suspect Brian has hypnotised her. When we used her name, she obeyed unquestioningly. And when I read certain phrases from the letter she performed certain actions. They must be cues.'

'But is it possible to hypnotise someone by letter?' asked Jemma.

'I doubt it,' said Raphael. 'I suspect Brian hypnotised Maddy in person before he left to challenge me. If he lost, that was his last chance to influence the bookshop. If I lost, it would be easy for him to return and bring Maddy round.'

Jemma gasped. 'That's so sneaky,' she said. 'But it's an awful lot of trouble to take, just to inconvenience us.'

'I don't think it's that,' said Raphael. 'As he's been sending his friends round to spy, I think there's more to it. I'm hoping Maddy will tell us.'

Maddy returned with a tray full of mugs a few minutes later. 'Thank you, Maddy,' said Raphael. 'Please take a seat. I'd like to talk to you, if I may.'

'Of course,' she said, sitting down.

'Maddy, sleep,' said Raphael, making a movement with his hand.

Maddy stared at him. 'I'm sorry, what did you say?'

'I just wondered if there were any biscuits, Maddy,' said Raphael.

'I'll go and see,' said Maddy. Her chair scraped back.

'She's resisting me,' said Raphael, when she had gone. 'I don't know if Brian has built that in, or if she doesn't trust me. She doesn't know me very well.'

'She probably doesn't trust me either,' said Jemma. She thought for a moment. 'I might be able to help. Hold the fort, I'll fetch Luke.'

'Luke?' said Raphael. 'Really?'

Jemma turned to him. 'Have you got any better ideas?'

'Well, no, but who will run the shop? Carl will be on his own.' Then Raphael's face cleared. 'Got it.'

They jumped to their feet just as Maddy returned with a biscuit barrel. 'Maddy, stay put,' Raphael said. 'We'll be back in a couple of minutes.' They ran out of the shop as Maddy, still clutching the biscuits, gazed after them.

'You get Luke,' Raphael panted, as they jogged down the road. 'I have something to do first.' He stopped, straightened his tie, and opened the door to Rolando's.

Jemma stopped dead. 'Raphael, we don't have time for coffee!'

'I'll see you in two minutes,' shouted Raphael. 'Don't worry.'

Jemma sighed, and hurried on.

***

'What's up?' said Luke. 'You two dashed out of here as

if the police were after you.'

'Not this time,' said Jemma. 'We need you.'

'Me? What about the shop?'

'Raphael's sorting it,' Jemma said. 'Don't ask how.'

'OK,' said Luke, 'but what do you need me for?'

'Tell you when we get there,' said Jemma. 'Actually, can you go downstairs and tell Carl you're coming with us? And – and give him my love.'

Luke raised his eyebrows. 'Isn't that your job?'

'Oh, for heaven's sake,' said Jemma. 'If you want anything done properly—' She scowled at him and ran downstairs.

The queue at the café counter was long; early birds were already ordering lunch. Carl saw her and waved. Jemma ran straight towards him, and he looked rather alarmed. 'I'm a bit busy—'

'I don't care,' said Jemma, and threw her arms round him. 'Brian's messing about again. Raphael and I need to deal with him, and I don't even know what that means yet. But I love you, and I had to tell you.' And she kissed him. From behind her came whistles and cheers, along with comments about jumping the queue, but she didn't let it interrupt her very important business.

Finally she had to come up for air. She looked at Carl, embarrassed, but not at all sorry.

'If this is what happens when Brian messes about,' Carl murmured, 'I kind of wish he'd do it more often.' And then it was his turn to kiss her.

They broke off at an extremely loud throat-clearing and found Giulia watching them, arms folded, and managing somehow to combine a glare and a twinkle. 'Business first, Carl,' she said, 'fun afterwards.'

'Quite,' said Raphael. 'I've explained to Luke, and while we're gone Giulia will be in charge.'

Carl saluted both of them. 'Yes, boss.' He gave Jemma a final squeeze, then let her go. 'I'll see you later,' he said.

'Yes,' said Jemma, 'you will.' She wished she felt as confident as she sounded.

***

They found Maddy where they had left her, still holding the biscuit barrel. 'Maddy,' said Raphael, 'you may put the biscuits down now.'

Maddy put the biscuits on the counter.

'She's exhausted,' said Luke.

Jemma glanced at him, then at Maddy. 'You're right,' she said. 'Now you've said that, it's so obvious.'

'Take a seat, Maddy,' said Raphael. 'You may sit next to Luke.'

She eyed Luke, then looked away.

'Please, Maddy,' said Luke. 'I'd like you to sit next to me.'

The faintest flush of pink appeared in Maddy's pale cheeks. Slowly, she walked towards him and sat down.

'That's right,' said Luke, and patted her arm.

'Are you tired, Maddy?' asked Raphael.

She gazed at him. 'Yes,' she murmured.

'Would you like to sleep, Maddy?' He made a pass with his hand. Her eyelids flickered, then opened.

'It's all right, Maddy,' said Luke. He put his hand on hers. 'You're safe. You can sleep.'

She looked at him, and Jemma saw the hint of a smile on her face. Raphael made the gesture again, and her eyes slowly closed. 'Tell me about Brian, Maddy.'

'I knew he would challenge you,' she said, dreamily. 'He spoke of practically nothing else. He said that if you won you would ruin the bookshop, and he would arrange insurance just in case. Then one day he came out of the stockroom, where he'd been rearranging books – I don't know why, everything was in order – and told me I had to listen carefully. The next thing I knew he was gone, and he didn't come back. Ever since, I haven't felt quite myself. I stop in the middle of doing something and can't remember why I'm doing it. I don't sleep well; I wake in the night worrying about the shop. And Jemma's angry with me so often. I try my best, but sometimes I do the wrong things. I think it's because I'm not concentrating.'

Raphael and Jemma exchanged glances. 'Maddy, Brian writes to you, doesn't he?'

'Yes, Mr Burns,' said Maddy. 'Only short letters, but it's nice to hear from him. He writes quite often.'

'So that's how he's doing it,' said Jemma. 'He's prompting her behaviour by letter.' Her fists clenched.

'Maddy, can you remember which books Brian moved?' asked Raphael.

'I can't,' said Maddy. 'But he told me that if I found a book out of place in the stockroom, I was to leave it where it was and update the database.'

'Jemma, can you get into the database?' said Raphael.

'Yes,' said Jemma. 'I'll take a look.' She moved to the counter, typed in the password, and began scrolling.

'Maddy, listen,' said Raphael. 'None of this is your fault. Do you understand?'

Maddy smiled, her eyes still closed. 'Is that true?'

'Yes, it is,' said Raphael.

'Of course it is,' added Luke, and squeezed her hand.

'I've found something,' said Jemma. 'Three books about technical interference, and three about signal jamming, shelved on either side of the communication section.' She took her phone out of her pocket and looked at it. 'My phone hasn't picked up messages for ages...'

'See what happens if you put them back in the right place,' said Raphael. 'I'll keep talking to Maddy.'

'I can go, if you want,' said Luke.

'You're busy here,' said Raphael. 'Besides, this is a job for an Assistant Keeper.'

Jemma went into the stockroom. For the first time she was pleased it was so much smaller than the one at Burns Books; it made everything easier to find. She found the first three books easily. They were slightly pulled out, as if Brian dared her to move them.

Jemma took a step towards the books, and tried to take another, but her foot wouldn't move. *Let me do this.* 'I am an Assistant Keeper,' she said aloud. She took a step, and her hand closed on the first book. A shock like static ran through her and she yelped, but she managed to pull it out. She took it to its rightful place, and couldn't help sighing with relief as she pushed it home. The second book was less painful, and the third felt like moving any book between any pair of shelves. And as Jemma moved the second trio of books, she noted how the closeness in the stockroom had lifted.

As Jemma pulled the last book from the shelf, her phone buzzed and buzzed. She took it from her pocket, and as the screen filled with the messages that had been held back for so long, her eyes filled with tears. She blinked hard, and put her phone away. *I can catch up with it all later.*

'Did it work?' asked Raphael, when she returned.

'Yes,' she said, sitting at the computer. 'I'll keep looking.'

Raphael turned back to Maddy. 'You're sure there's nothing else you can tell us, Maddy?'

'I don't think so,' said Maddy. 'Except that Brian invited his friends here in the evenings, and he was always very smug and energetic the next day. He'd say bookselling ought to be more strictly regulated, and we needed more rules. I generally humoured him.'

'I don't believe it,' murmured Jemma. 'I've just found loads of books on financial mismanagement sandwiching the business section. No wonder it's been so hard to get the shop to make a decent profit.' She stood up.

'Wait,' said Raphael. 'Maddy, do you know where Brian is?'

'No,' said Maddy. 'Sorry.'

'You're sure?'

'Yes, I'm sure. His letters aren't postmarked, and he said before he went that if he had to leave, he'd go where no one could find him.'

Raphael sighed. 'Thank you, Maddy.' He looked at the others. 'I'm going to bring Maddy round. Keep holding her hand, Luke.' He leaned forward. 'Maddy,' he said, gently. 'You've helped us a great deal, and I know you've done your best. When I wake you up, that will end Brian's hold over you. If you ever receive another letter from him, don't open it. Give it to Jemma, or me. Do you understand?'

'I understand.'

'And will you do as I ask?'

'Yes.'

'Good,' said Raphael. 'Maddy, Brian is no longer your employer, and he has no hold over you.' He paused. 'It's time for you to wake up.'

Maddy's eyes pinged open. She stared at Raphael, then at her surroundings, and her eyes grew rounder and rounder. She took in the piles of books by the door and put a hand to her mouth. 'Did I do that?' she asked, in a shocked whisper.

'Yes,' said Jemma, 'but you couldn't help it. I understand now. I'm so sorry, Maddy.'

Maddy blinked at her. Her shoulders tensed, then suddenly she was shaking with sobs. 'It was him, wasn't it?' she cried, between gulps and wails. 'He said you'd lower the bookshop's standards and corrupt me, and that he'd stop you if it was the last thing he did! He said that the happiest day of his life would be when he read your obituary in the *Bookseller's Companion.* I told him how wrong those thoughts were, but—'

Luke moved closer and put his arms around her. 'Don't worry, Maddy, it's all right,' he murmured. 'You're free of him now. We'll make sure he can never do this to you or anyone else ever again.' He looked at Raphael. 'Won't we?'

'Yes,' said Raphael, rather uncertainly. 'Yes, we shall.'

'But how?' said Jemma. 'We don't know where he is.'

'I can guess,' said Raphael. 'He's barred from Westminster, and he won't be able to bear being far from books.' He sat up straight. 'Luke, stay here, look after Maddy, and mind the bookshop until we get back. Jemma and I must track Brian down and finish this.'

'Where are we going?' said Jemma. 'Do I need to pack?'

Raphael grinned. 'Perhaps a coat. We're going to the town of books: Hay-on-Wye.'

Chapter 19

'This will take hours,' said Jemma, gazing at the maps app on her phone. 'I know London was quiet, but it's such a long way to the Welsh border. The bookshops will probably be closed by the time we get there.'

'Don't you worry about that,' said Raphael. 'Gertrude's got a good turn of speed when she puts her mind to it.'

'Yes,' said Jemma, 'I gathered.' She had found herself clinging to the handle above the passenger door as Raphael navigated the back streets of London, twisting this way and that until she felt dizzy and nauseous. No hairpin was too tight for Gertrude, no alley too narrow. 'Out of interest, Raphael, have you ever been stopped by the police when you're out in Gertrude?'

'Nope,' said Raphael. 'But if you distract me by talking too much, there's always a first time.'

Jemma subsided into silence, and tried to relax as

Raphael took the slip road to the motorway. *I do hope he'll observe the speed limit.* That was a minor worry compared to what would happen once they got to Hay-on-Wye. Would they be able to find Brian? And if so, what then?

She had thought Raphael would at least pack books for the journey, in case of another battle of knowledge. However, all he had brought was an overcoat, a multicoloured stripy scarf, a flask of coffee, and a bag of cinnamon buns. 'The essentials,' he said, passing the flask and the buns to Jemma. 'We may not be able to stop for lunch.'

At the last minute he had run up to his flat, and come out holding a small, strange contraption which Jemma thought she had seen on his shelves. It was made of metal, covered in black enamel, and featured several intersecting cogs and a handle. Jemma had no idea what it was for, and she really didn't want to ask. She remembered Raphael and Brian's previous confrontation, when she had been convinced that Raphael had lost, and fretted. What if Brian's powers had grown? What if his enchantments had affected Raphael's powers?

Suddenly Gertrude shot forward, and Jemma's back pressed into her seat. Jolted out of her thoughts, she stared at the road ahead, which was advancing at a ridiculous speed. 'Slow down, Raphael!' she cried. 'We'll get pulled over! Or we could die!'

'Don't know what you mean,' said Raphael. 'I'm doing a steady seventy, and the conditions are perfect.'

'I know what seventy miles an hour feels like,' said Jemma, through gritted teeth, 'and this is not it.' A police car pulled alongside. 'See, I told you.'

Raphael raised a hand to the police officer in the passenger seat, who waved back. The police car pulled ahead of them, indicated, and moved into the exit slip road. 'See? Nothing to worry about,' said Raphael.

'Have we got any cinnamon rolls left?' asked Jemma.

'Yes, plenty,' said Raphael. 'Would you like one? It might take your mind off things.'

'Not right now,' said Jemma. 'But I may need the bag.' She pointed at the speedometer, whose needle pointed at the number 70. 'Is that thing working?'

'Oh yes,' said Raphael. 'We are doing seventy. It's just that the motorway happens to be doing sixty-five in the opposite direction.'

Jemma closed her eyes. 'That makes me feel so much better.'

'Oh good,' said Raphael. 'If you don't mind, we'd better stop chatting so that I can concentrate on the road.'

Jemma fell silent, and lapsed into an uneasy mixture of looking at the road ahead, wishing she hadn't, and pondering what might happen. 'Can I ask you something?'

'You may,' said Raphael, his eyes on the road, 'but I don't guarantee an answer.'

'How come we haven't brought the others with us?' asked Jemma. 'Last time you and Brian faced off, Carl and Luke were there too.'

'They were,' said Raphael. 'This is different. For one thing, there's Maddy to consider. I couldn't possibly bring her anywhere near Brian.'

Jemma gasped. 'You mean that Brian might harm her?'

'There is that,' said Raphael. 'But I'm also worried that she might harm Brian. I have a feeling that the extreme upset and disgust that Maddy experienced when we brought her round could easily turn into rage. And anyway, it isn't her job to deal with Brian. In the first instance, it's mine.'

'Yes, but we could have sent her home,' said Jemma. 'Or Luke could have looked after her, and Carl could have come with us. I know it would mean closing the bookshop, but—'

'That isn't the reason,' said Raphael. 'The challenge you observed has strict rules. This is entirely different, and I would never risk bringing anyone ranked lower than Assistant Keeper to assist at a confrontation such as this.'

'But I'm only acting,' said Jemma. 'I'm not qualified!'

'You were qualified enough to remove Brian's enchantments from your shop,' said Raphael. 'You undid the work of an Assistant Keeper, as he was when he undertook it. You are more than qualified, and I have every faith in you.'

'I don't,' mumbled Jemma.

'Well, I do,' said Raphael, 'and that's the end of it. Now do be quiet; we are coming off the motorway, and I always take the wrong road at this point if I'm not careful.'

Gertrude slowed to something approaching normal speed, then picked up the pace as they took an A road. Another motorway followed; Jemma had given up even trying to navigate. Eventually Raphael turned onto a narrower country road, and Jemma breathed a sigh of relief as Gertrude's engine modulated from a roar to a purr. She looked at the clock set into Gertrude's dashboard. Ten past one. 'We've made good time,' she said, weakly.

'We have,' said Raphael.

They drove on, and Gertrude seemed to crawl along. More houses appeared and they eased into a town. A sign read first *Y GELLI: tref y llyfrau*, then *HAY-ON-WYE: town of books*. Jemma felt a little pull at her heart, as if someone had plucked it like the string on a guitar. She shivered.

Raphael glanced across. 'You can feel it too,' he said. 'Never tell me that you're not qualified again.'

They drove on, and came to a fork in the road. 'Left or right?' asked Raphael.

'Left,' said Jemma, though she could not have said why. Her heart trembled, and she couldn't tell if it were from anticipation or fear.

They joined a queue of traffic. 'Let's find a car park,' said Raphael. 'The rest will be easier on foot. Here we are.' He indicated, manoeuvred Gertrude under the barrier, and parked. 'I'll get a ticket.'

Jemma held up her right hand, which trembled slightly. Her left did, too. She was about to rub her face when she remembered she was still wearing the make-up she had put on for the meeting. *Maybe I can scare Brian into submission*, she thought, with a wry smile. Then she looked around. To the left seemed fine; to the right, that twanging feeling.

Her door opened. 'I've got two hours,' said Raphael, 'that ought to be enough. Let's go and get this over with. Oh, wait a minute—' He reached into the inner pocket of his jacket and brought out two pencils, one of which he handed to Jemma. Then he fished out the small metal contraption and put it on Gertrude's dashboard. 'Excuse the mess.' He inserted his pencil into the device, turned the handle, and wooden shavings spilled out.

Jemma stared. 'You brought a *pencil sharpener*?'

Raphael drew out the pencil, now very sharp, and regarded it critically. 'I hope we won't need these, but it's always best to be prepared.' He held his hand out, and Jemma passed him her pencil.

'What am I supposed to do with this?' she asked, when he passed it back.

'If you need to use it,' said Raphael, 'you'll know. Which way?'

'Right,' said Jemma.

She led the way, following the feeling, turning left, then left again. The feeling pulsed inside her, then strengthened suddenly as they approached an alley. Jemma swallowed.

'Take deep breaths if you're worried,' said Raphael. 'Don't let it get the better of you.'

Jemma did as Raphael instructed, taking slow, deep breaths as she walked along. Eventually they came out of the alley, and without hesitation Jemma turned right. She stopped outside a small, ramshackle shop, whose sign said *Curious Books and Antiquities*. 'I think this is it,' she said.

'I think you're right,' said Raphael. 'Got your pencil?'

Jemma rummaged in her pocket and held it up.

'Good. Then in we go.' And he pushed open the door.

A bell jangled, and Jemma felt almost reassured. The shop was dim, shabby, quaint. She could see why Brian had been drawn to it. But the cheerful young man who materialised from behind a curtain to greet them was not Brian. 'Hello, how may I help you?' he asked.

'I wondered if I might speak to your assistant,' said Raphael. 'Is he about?'

'Yes, and no,' said the young man. 'He is in, but he's having his lunch. I can see if he's free, if you like.'

'That would be most helpful,' said Raphael.

The young man vanished and they heard the murmur of voices in the back room. Raphael delved into his pocket and pulled out, of all things, a mobile phone. 'Ten to two,' he commented, peering at it. 'Hopefully we can get things sorted in time for a late lunch.' He pushed a button on the phone and put it in his pocket. 'If we don't, I doubt that either of us will want lunch anyway.'

'Don't cheer me up with too much positivity, will you,' said Jemma. She was still trying to take deep, slow breaths, but finding it difficult. She gazed around her to calm herself, and jumped at the sight of a familiar book; hardback, green cloth, with gilt detailing. 'The *Origin of Species*!' she cried, clutching Raphael's arm. 'Drusilla bought it for him!' Then her heart leapt into her throat as the curtain twitched, and a familiar figure appeared.

Chapter 20

A familiar figure, and yet not. In the few months since she had last seen him, Brian's stoop had become more pronounced. His hair was thinner, his face more deeply lined. *He's grown older*, she thought, trying not to stare. *Much, much older.*

'Ah, there you are, Brian,' said Raphael, as if Brian had popped into the back half an hour ago. 'How are you enjoying your new employment?'

'It keeps me busy,' said Brian. He struggled to look Raphael in the eye now, but his eyes were the same bold, defiant blue. *Mysterious blue*, thought Jemma.

'I wasn't referring to your work in this bookshop,' said Raphael. 'I meant your extra-curricular activities. Specifically, sending your cronies to spy on Jemma here, booby-trapping her bookshop, and last but not least, putting your poor ex-assistant under a hypnotic enchantment. What do you have to say for yourself?'

'The Keepers' Guild always upholds the rights of the individual,' said Brian, drawing himself up as tall as he could. 'The right of the individual member to challenge whomever he likes; the right of an individual member to maintain his bookshop as he sees fit. How I arrange the books in my shop is my concern. How I manage my staff is my concern. And if people who may know me choose to visit a bookshop, that's hardly unusual. If that's all you've come for, I suggest you browse in the shop, see if there's anything you wish to buy, then return to London. I have nothing to say to you.' He shuffled towards the curtain.

'Wait a moment,' said Raphael. He pulled out his pencil, and pointed it at Brian's back.

Brian stopped dead.

Raphael drew a slow circle in the air, and Brian began to turn. He resisted every movement, but despite his struggles, in a few seconds he was facing Raphael again.

Raphael advanced to the counter and rested the point of his pencil on it. 'It isn't very nice to feel as if you're out of your own control, is it, Brian?' he said.

Brian glared at him but did not move, and Jemma realised that he couldn't.

'Jemma, take out your pencil,' said Raphael.

She looked at him doubtfully, but obeyed.

'Brian, if I were cruel, I would instruct Jemma to make you dance to her tune,' said Raphael. 'However, luckily for you, I am not a cruel man, and I have no wish to wear out your old bones any more than necessary.' He pointed with the pencil to a chair. 'Sit.'

Brian shambled over to the chair and sat, glowering. 'You'll get nothing out of me,' he said.

'You have already told me that, Brian,' said Raphael. 'There is no point in repeating it. Jemma, would you mind doing something for me? There is a notepad by the cash register. I would like you to write, as concisely as you can, what Brian has done to hamper your management of the Friendly Bookshop.'

Brian winced. 'I tell you I've done nothing—'

Jemma pointed her pencil at Brian and he was immediately silent. She glanced at Raphael. 'Please, write,' he said.

And Jemma wrote.

Brian, former Assistant Keeper for Westminster, hypnotised Maddy Shenton, assistant at the Friendly Bookshop. He did this with the intention of controlling her, and forcing her to perform actions which would impede the bookshop's business. After the initial hypnosis, he controlled her by means of regular letters. We know this both from Maddy's testimony and our own observations.

Brian also arranged books in the stockroom to thwart the business and block communications: specifically, texts and calls. I removed these arrangements, and communications were restored immediately.

It is also likely that Brian instructed friends of his to visit the bookshop, report back, and acquire books from it. These friends are known sympathisers of Brian, and they have stirred up trouble and disrupted Raphael's work. I cannot confirm this without further investigation.

She showed Raphael. 'Will that do?'

Raphael scanned the page. 'That seems fair-minded and well-evidenced,' he said. 'Your penmanship needs improvement, but you can't have everything.' He pushed the notepad back to her. 'Please sign it and add the date and your title, and then I have a little to add.'

Jemma signed her name, with the little flourish that she always added, and printed it underneath. She added the date, then wrote *Assistant Keeper*. After it she drew a bracket, then began to write the A of *Acting*, but a tiny piece of the pencil lead broke off. 'Darn,' she said.

'Don't worry about it,' said Raphael, 'just rub out the bracket. It will do as it is.'

'But—'

'Trust me.' Raphael took the notepad and wrote rapidly beneath Jemma's script. *I certify that this is a true account, evidenced, and written moreover with a Pencil of Truth, as is this statement. Raphael Burns, Keeper of England.* He held the notepad up for Brian to see. 'Can you deny any of this?'

'No,' said Brian, 'and I don't wish to.'

'Oh dear,' said Raphael. 'Never mind, eh?'

Brian grinned, showing crooked teeth with one missing from the bottom row. 'Is that all you've got? Some scribbles with a so-called magic pencil?'

'I also have this.' Raphael held up his mobile phone. 'Nifty, isn't it?'

Brian's grin broadened. 'What will you do, dial 999?'

'Oh, I can do better than that,' said Raphael. He pressed a button and took a picture first of the notepad, then of

Brian. His fingers moved over the screen, and they heard a whoosh.

'Aren't you supposed to ask permission before you take pictures of people?' said Brian, frowning.

'Usually, yes,' said Raphael. 'But I'm pretty sure there's an exception when you're either investigating or preventing crime. Isn't there?' he asked the phone.

'Indeed there is,' the phone replied, and Jemma jumped. There, filling the screen, was the face of a man who seemed middle-aged, but for a shock of white hair. His expression appeared neutral, but every so often a ripple of anger disturbed it.

'Jemma, may I introduce Armand Dupont, Head of European Operations for the Keepers' Guild,' said Raphael. 'Armand, this is Jemma James, Assistant Keeper for Westminster until the vacancy is filled.'

'Delighted,' said Armand Dupont. He spoke in perfect, unaccented English. 'Thank you for dialling me in earlier, Raphael. It has been a most interesting conversation. Could you turn me to face Brian, please.'

Brian's lower lip trembled and he edged backwards, seeming to shrink into his chair. 'Please… I did nothing wrong.'

'Oh, but you did,' said Armand Dupont. 'You are correct in that you may arrange your bookshop as you like, and manage your assistant as you see fit. However, those rights end from the moment the bookshop ceases to be yours. By deliberately putting those precautions in place, you were violating the rights which you spoke of so self-righteously earlier. And by hypnotising your assistant, who is also an associate of the Guild, you violated *her* rights. Impeding the operations of a bookshop under the auspices of the Guild is absolutely forbidden, and carries a heavy punishment.'

'I'm sorry!' cried Brian. 'I didn't know!'

'In your heart, you knew,' the remorseless voice continued. 'But you chose to misinterpret the rules; to observe the letter and ignore the spirit. You chose to remain wilfully ignorant. In doing so, you disrupted the work of one of the highest-ranking officials of the Guild, and you also caused me inconvenience. I can't decide which of these things displeases me more. But I digress. Raphael, could you turn me back to your Assistant Keeper, please?'

As Raphael did so, they heard a low mutter, 'Why couldn't the man use a laptop, for heaven's sake? Or even a tablet.' Jemma straightened her face hastily as the phone found her. 'As a member of the Guild, you of all of us have suffered the most severe injury from Brian's actions. What do you think would be an appropriate punishment?'

'Oh, um, I don't know,' said Jemma. 'I mean, he's already banished.' Then a thought occurred to her. 'Hang on, is he a member of the Guild any more? Can you punish him?'

'Once a member, always a member,' said Armand Dupont. 'What do you feel is appropriate?'

Jemma bit her lip. *That applies to me, too. I'll always be a member of the Guild.* She wasn't sure whether to be pleased or worried. 'His punishment should stop him doing things like this,' she said. 'He is very old.' She remembered how he had been silenced by her pencil. 'And quite weak,' she added.

'That is true,' said Armand Dupont. 'But as we can see, still capable of venom. Raphael, what do you think?'

'I agree with Jemma,' said Raphael, giving Brian a pitying look. 'When Brian had power, he used it to attempt to overthrow and destroy. He acted in his own interests, not those of the Guild. But I believe we should be as merciful as we possibly can.'

'I concur,' said the phone. 'Brian, this is my decision. You may no longer approach or speak to another Guild member or associate, whether face to face or by means of technology. I shall also prevent you from handling books or communications technology with any malign intent. If you attempt it, you will suffer. Do I make myself clear?'

Already Brian seemed smaller, more wizened and shrunken. 'Yes,' he croaked.

'Good,' said Armand Dupont. 'Those measures are in force as of *now*.' He snapped his fingers.

Brian shrieked and hid his face. He peeped at Raphael and Jemma, screamed, and hobbled into the back room as fast as his legs could carry him. The curtain rippled for a moment, and then the folds settled and became motionless, as if Brian had been swallowed by a merciless sea.

Jemma and Raphael looked at each other, then at the phone. 'That seems to have worked,' said Raphael.

'Yes,' said Armand Dupont. 'I apologise for that letter, by the way. I was dealing with an incident in a library in Paris, you see, and you caught me at a bad time. Now I see what has been going on, I completely understand.

Skulduggery is absolutely a tactic of the Guild, but not when it undermines our own business.'

'Quite,' said Raphael. 'Well, now that's all settled, Jemma and I might have lunch.'

For the first time, Armand Dupont's face showed strong emotion. 'You haven't had lunch? What were you thinking of? How could you even contemplate undertaking tasks such as this on an empty stomach? Go and remedy this matter immediately. Oh yes, and it was nice to meet you . . . Jemma, was it?'

'That's right,' said Jemma. 'Jemma James.'

'Jemma James. I shall remember. Go and have a nice lunch, and don't forget to charge it to expenses.' His brow furrowed. 'Are you in Hay-on-Wye?'

'Yes,' said Jemma, 'we are.'

'Ah, Hay-on-Wye…' A dreamy expression came over his face. 'Oh, to be browsing, free from care.' He smiled, and suddenly looked younger still. 'Enjoy your afternoon. Au revoir.' His face disappeared, replaced by a blank screen.

Jemma stared at Raphael. 'Is that it? We've done it?'

'No,' said Raphael. 'We haven't done it. *You've* done it. You did pretty much all of it. You noted unusual phenomena, alerted your manager, and detected and removed misused knowledge sources without personal protective equipment.' He held up his pencil, and a faint wail came from the back room. 'You tracked down a felon, bore effective witness using a Pencil of Truth, and recommended mercy, as an Assistant Keeper should.' He sighed. 'You do realise this means I shall have to write a report, don't you.'

'But not yet,' said Jemma. 'Come on, let's get out of here.' She noticed, with great relief, that the fear and apprehension she had felt earlier had completely vanished. 'I feel better than I have in weeks.'

'You know what,' said Raphael, 'so do I.'

'We must tell the others,' said Jemma, as they walked along the main street, looking for restaurants.

'Oh yes,' said Raphael. 'But not until we've ordered.'

Chapter 21

Carl appeared from behind one of the screens which was acting as the wings, and faced the applauding audience. 'We will now have a half-hour interval. Refreshments are available from the café.' He waved a hand at the café counter, towards which Giulia was hurrying. 'The bathrooms are in the corner. I'll come out again and give you a five-minute warning to resume your seats. Thank you for your attention.'

'It's going well, isn't it?' Raphael murmured to Jemma.

She beamed with pride. 'Yes, it is. I'll nip backstage and check on Carl. I don't suppose you could get me a cappuccino?'

Raphael stood up and stretched. 'On it,' he said, and ambled over to the forming queue.

Jemma nudged Luke, who was sitting on her other side. 'What do you think?' she whispered.

'What? Oh yes, it's very good. Isn't it, Maddy?'

Maddy looked enraptured, although Jemma suspected that was more to do with sitting next to Luke than the premiere of Carl's play. 'Oh yes, it's delightful.'

'I'll pass that on to Carl,' said Jemma. 'See you after the interval.'

Maddy's right, she thought. *It's really, really good. And thoroughly deserved; they've worked so hard on it.*

Now that things were running more smoothly at the Friendly Bookshop, she had attended a few rehearsals as an 'average spectator'. 'I want this to be the sort of play that anyone could enjoy,' Carl had said. 'Not just people who go to the theatre all the time and know what to expect. I want someone who maybe goes once a year or less to get something out of this play.' He looked rather fierce as he said it.

'Well, that's me,' Jemma had replied. 'I can't remember the last time I went to the theatre.' She thought for a moment. 'That ought to change. Now the bookshop is behaving more or less as it should, I can have hobbies. I can go out in the evening and enjoy myself.' She gave him a playful nudge. 'That's if I can get you to come with me, of course, when you're not rehearsing.'

Carl had laughed. 'I daresay I'll be at a loose end soon enough. We're only doing three performances, then we'll probably be hustling again.' But somehow, Jemma suspected he wouldn't have to hustle too hard.

She walked to the screen and stuck her head round it. 'Is it OK to come in?'

Carl turned. 'Do you think it's going all right?'

Jemma spread her hands. 'Didn't you hear the applause? Didn't you hear them laughing in all the places you wanted them to?'

Carl looked slightly less anxious. 'I suppose. But I worry.'

'Of course,' said Jemma, 'and that's normal, but everyone's enjoying it.' She moved closer and wrapped her arms around him. 'You've done such a brilliant job. Your first play, and the audience love it.'

'There's the second half yet,' said Carl, still appearing a little uneasy. 'Don't jinx it.'

'I won't,' she said, and kissed him.

A couple of cast members wandered over. 'Sorry to interrupt, Carl, but have you got any notes for us?' said one.

'Sure, give me two seconds,' said Carl. He looked at Jemma. 'Sorry.'

'Don't apologise,' said Jemma. 'You're doing your job.' She stroked his cheek. 'I'll see you afterwards.'

As Carl beckoned to the rest of the cast, Jemma lingered behind the screen, gazing at the lower floor of the bookshop. They had sold out the venue, a hundred seats, and they were packed to capacity. In the third row – 'we don't want to be too conspicuous' – were her mum and dad. Even from this distance she could hear her mother talking to someone in the second row. 'It's excellent, isn't it? My daughter is the playwright's partner—' She spotted Jemma and waved, then stuck two thumbs up. 'And Debra is his mum…' Debra, sitting next to her, smiled politely, but underneath Jemma could tell that she was bursting with pride.

Some of the audience would be friends and family of the cast, of course, but she could also see a few bookshop regulars. The two Golden Age crime ladies were there, and Mohammed, in the third row, studying his programme. And was she mistaken, or were Felicity and Jerome whispering together at the back?

Speaking of together, Luke and Maddy seemed very happy. They weren't going out exactly, but Luke had expressed an interest in spending time at the Friendly Bookshop to learn more about antiquarian books from Maddy. Since this freed Jemma to spend more time at Burns Books with Raphael and Carl, she had ordered more sunlight-filtering window film and been only too happy to agree.

Once Maddy had recovered from her anger and distress at the ordeal she had been through, with Luke acting as a sort of unofficial therapist, she had made a proposition to Jemma. 'We have all these valuable books in the stockroom,' she said, waving a hand at it in a dismissive way that Jemma could not have imagined a few weeks ago. 'Now that – things have changed, and the fiction section is doing so well, it makes sense to extend it. But at the same time, it's silly to ignore the stuff we have. Why don't we sort of split the bookshop in half? You put more of your books out, and I work with the existing books.' She gazed at Jemma, her anxiety visible on her face.

'That's a really good idea,' said Jemma. 'Let's draw up a plan, try it for a month, and see how things go.'

Already, the idea was bearing fruit. The people who

wanted non-fiction in posh bindings flocked to Maddy, and those seeking good-quality fiction made a beeline for Jemma – or Luke, if he was in. Often Jemma would return from lunch, or from the other shop, and find Luke and Maddy having an animated discussion about *Seven Gothic Tales*, or which was the best film version of *Dracula*.

'Don't you find the age difference a problem?' she asked Luke once, when they were in the back room making tea.

Luke considered for a moment, then shook his head. 'I know I'm a lot older than Maddy,' he said, 'but she is so wise when you get past her shy exterior. I don't see it as a problem at all.'

Jemma looked at the café counter, where Raphael was laughing with Giulia as she made his drinks. They had arrived together, too. She wasn't sure if that meant anything, or if it would continue, but she hoped it did. *He deserves happiness as much as anyone.*

A chirrup made her look down. Folio, wearing a smart collar for the occasion, was rubbing against her leg. She scratched him behind the ears. 'Are you enjoying the play?' Folio had been allocated his own seat in the front row, and when she glanced at him from time to time, he was paying attention, his head moving as the different actors spoke. She had been slightly worried that he might attempt to become part of the proceedings, but so far he had behaved very well.

Folio chirruped again, which she presumed was a yes, then ran towards the café area, pulling up next to Raphael. Raphael murmured something to Giulia, who laughed.

'I thought it was you!'

Jemma jumped. A small pink-haired woman had materialised beside her. 'Stella!' she exclaimed. 'You came!'

'Oh yes,' said Stella. 'I've never attended a first night before, and it's ever so good. Do you think I could maybe speak to some of the cast? I want to write this up on my blog.'

'I'm sure that would be fine,' said Jemma. 'You know Carl, don't you? He's the writer and director.' She pointed to where Carl was talking with the cast, gesturing occasionally. Just then his hands fell to his sides, and the cast began to drift away. 'Now looks like a good time, if you're quick.'

'I shall be quick,' said Stella, and bustled away. A couple of minutes later, a tall man with an interesting beard, wearing jeans, a fisherman's sweater, and an artfully-draped scarf, wandered over to join them. 'Promising first half,' he declared, extending a hand and at the same time holding up a card. 'Henry Sims, drama critic at the *Evening Clarion*.'

Carl's face lit up, and Jemma's heart filled on his behalf.

And what about me? Well, I have Carl, and there's the flat to redecorate, and the bookshop is flying–

And the other thing? her inner voice prompted.

Yes, my mum finally understands that I'm serious about the bookshop, and she's happy–

You know exactly what I mean.

Jemma smiled. She had applied for the post of

Assistant Keeper, on the grounds that it wouldn't hurt, and the closing date was tomorrow. She had handed her application to Raphael herself. 'Although now I know how tech-savvy you are,' she said, 'I could have emailed it, couldn't I?'

Raphael looked shamefaced. 'Sometimes it pays to have a little in reserve,' he said. 'Anyway, I'm glad you've applied.'

'Have you had much interest?' asked Jemma.

'Are you fishing, Jemma?' Raphael laughed. 'Not a great deal. Those in the know are aware that there is a very strong candidate in the field whom they don't want to go up against.'

Jemma grimaced. 'It isn't Drusilla, is it? I don't think I could bear her being any closer than she is.'

Raphael gazed at her with something like affection. 'For someone so smart and talented, Jemma James, you really can be an absolute chump. I mean you.'

'Me?' said Jemma. 'But I—'

'Remember in Hay-on-Wye—'

'I know, I helped with sorting out Brian,' said Jemma.

'If you'll let me finish,' said Raphael. 'Remember when your pencil broke?'

Jemma frowned. 'Yes, but I was probably pressing too hard.'

'What were you writing?'

It was like yesterday. Jemma could see it in her mind's eye: printing her name, writing *Assistant Keeper*, opening the bracket… 'I was about to write *Acting*.'

'Yes, and your lead broke, because a Pencil of Truth

can only write truth. You weren't *acting* as an Assistant Keeper; you were *being* an Assistant Keeper. There is an important distinction, and the Pencil of Truth never lies.' For a moment he looked like a wise old owl. 'That is all I shall say on the subject for now.'

Jemma remembered the flood of pride she had felt; but she also remembered her nausea when they were searching for Brian, and the shock that had gone through her when she removed that first enchanted book. *Can I really do it?* she thought. *Can I face that fear, possibly every day, and master it?*

'But wouldn't it be an adventure?' whispered her inner voice. 'Wouldn't it be an incredible adventure?'

Carl walked out of the wings and faced the audience, and Jemma strolled back to her front-row seat. Tonight there was the rest of the play to enjoy, and dinner with her family and Carl's. But then— She closed her eyes and imagined a strange and wonderful future rolling out ahead of her like a magic carpet. *Do I dare?* Her toes tingled with anticipation, and she smiled to herself.

Acknowledgements

As usual, my first thanks go to my wonderful beta readers – Carol Bissett, Ruth Cunliffe, Paula Harmon, and Stephen Lenhardt – and my meticulous proofreader, John Croall. As usual, any remaining errors are mine only. Thank you all for your support – and while Jemma and Raphael will be putting their feet up for a while, they may well return!

My husband Stephen gets additional thanks for his ongoing support and encouragement, which has been more valued than ever in these interesting times.

And my final thanks are for you, the reader. Thank you for reading, and I hope you enjoyed book 3! If you did, a short review or rating on Amazon or Goodreads would be very much appreciated. Ratings and reviews, however short, help readers to discover books.

FONT AND IMAGE CREDITS

Cover and heading fonts: Alyssum Blossom and Alyssum Blossom Sans by Bombastype

Houses: Set of hand drawn houses by freepik: https://www.freepik.com/free-vector/set-four-hand-drawn-houses_1926210.htm

Camper van: Vintage adventure logo collection by freepik: https://www.freepik.com/premium-vector/vintage-adventure-logo-collection_4400531.htm

Cat: Cats silhouettes pack vector by freepik at freepik.com: https://www.freepik.com/free-vector/cats-silhouettes-pack_719787.htm

Stars: Night free icon by flaticon at freepik.com: https://www.freepik.com/free-icon/night_914336.htm

Chapter vignette: Opened books in hand drawn style Free Vector by freepik at freepik.com: https://www.freepik.com/free-vector/opened-books-hand-drawn-style_765567.htm

Cover created using GIMP image editor: https://www.gimp.org

About the Author

Liz Hedgecock grew up in London, England, did an English degree, and then took forever to start writing. After several years working in the National Health Service, some short stories crept into the world. A few even won prizes. Then the stories started to grow longer…

Now Liz travels between the nineteenth and twenty-first centuries, murdering people. To be fair, she does usually clean up after herself.

Liz's reimaginings of Sherlock Holmes, her Pippa Parker cozy mystery series, the Caster & Fleet Victorian mystery series (written with Paula Harmon), and the Maisie Frobisher Mysteries are available in ebook and paperback.

Liz lives in Cheshire with her husband and two sons, and when she's not writing or child-wrangling you can usually find her reading, messing about on Twitter, or cooing over stuff in museums and art galleries. That's her story, anyway, and she's sticking to it.

Website/blog: http://lizhedgecock.wordpress.com
Facebook: http://www.facebook.com/lizhedgecockwrites
Twitter: http://twitter.com/lizhedgecock
Goodreads: https://www.goodreads.com/lizhedgecock
Amazon author page: http://author.to/LizH

Books by Liz Hedgecock

Short stories
The Secret Notebook of Sherlock Holmes
Bitesize
The Adventure of the Scarlet Rosebud

Halloween Sherlock series (novelettes)
The Case of the Snow-White Lady
Sherlock Holmes and the Deathly Fog
The Case of the Curious Cabinet

Sherlock & Jack series (novellas)
A Jar Of Thursday
Something Blue
A Phoenix Rises

Mrs Hudson & Sherlock Holmes series (novels)
A House Of Mirrors
In Sherlock's Shadow

Pippa Parker Mysteries (novels)
Murder At The Playgroup
Murder In The Choir
A Fete Worse Than Death
Murder in the Meadow
The QWERTY Murders
Past Tense

Caster & Fleet Mysteries (with Paula Harmon)
The Case of the Black Tulips
The Case of the Runaway Client
The Case of the Deceased Clerk
The Case of the Masquerade Mob
The Case of the Fateful Legacy
The Case of the Crystal Kisses

Maisie Frobisher Mysteries (novels)
All At Sea
Off The Map
Gone To Ground

The Magic Bookshop (short novels)
Every Trick in the Book
Brought to Book
Double Booked

For children (with Zoe Harmon)
A Christmas Carrot

183

Printed in Great Britain
by Amazon